HURMA

Ali al-Muqri is a Yemeni writer born in 1966. He has
worked in cultural journalism since 1985, has published
eight books including *Black Taste, Black Odour,* long-listed
for the International Prize for Arabic Fiction in 2009 and
The Handsome Jew, long-listed for the same prize in 2011.
His work has been translated into English, German, French
and Spanish.

ALI AL-MUQRI

HURMA

Translated by

T.M. Aplin

DARF PUBLISHERS
LONDON

Published by Darf Publishers 2015

Darf Publishers LTD, 277 West End Lane, London, NW6 1QS

Translated by T.M. Aplin
Cover by Luke Pajak

www.darfpublishers.co.uk

Twitter: @darfpublishers
ISBN 9781850772774
eBook ISBN 9781850772828

Printed and bound in Turkey by Mega Basim

Typeset by Palimpsest Book Production Limited, Falkirk, Stirlingshire

Side A of the Om Kalthoum tape

Ask my heart when it repents
Perhaps it will hold beauty to blame.

He gave me the cassette six years ago, but it's only now that I'm listening to it for the first time, having retrieved it from its hiding place in my old school bag. Back then the cover photo of the Egyptian singer, Om Kalthoum, and the title 'Ask My Heart,' were enough to stop me from even thinking of playing the cassette.

'I don't listen to songs,' I'd said to Suhail's sister that day, when she handed me the cassette, 'They're haram – they'll make God angry!'

But she insisted I keep it, afraid her brother would be upset if he knew I'd turned down his gift.

Ask my heart when it repents

Why did he give me this song? 'Repent' for what? Had Suhail repented? Is that why he rejected Laylat al-Qadr?

It never once crossed my mind that anyone would refuse Laylat al-Qadr, 'the Night of Destiny.' But then it happened to me. 'You'll regret it,' I told him, but he ignored me.

> *Ask a sensible man for sensible answers*
> *But who could keep his wits in the face of such beauty?*

It's obvious now that giving me the Om Kalthoum song – a song by 'the Diva' as my sister called her – was his way of flirting. But at the time I had no idea, because I didn't listen to it. I don't remember the last time I saw my body and my face in the mirror together. I look alluring, seductive. I've got a great waist, and what luscious lips! I don't know anyone else with such full breasts, and a bum as plump and peachy – how can any man resist? My body is still youthful. In my sheer nightie my reflection in the mirror is like a warm ocean, promising pleasure for any man who plunges into its waters. But . . . there's only me in the mirror.

The nearest man is Suhail, the next-door neighbour. Except for on Laylat al-Qadr, I don't think he'd ever seen me. Perhaps he'd caught the odd glimpse of me from afar, dressed in my long black coat or my loose cloak, my face hidden beneath my veil and headscarf. So the lyrics couldn't have been meant for me – unless perhaps he saw me in a dream? Don't some dreams come true, while most truths remain only dreams? Yes, that's it. He saw me in a dream, and became convinced that it was his Laylat al-Qadr.

> *If I were to ask my heart*
> *Tears would answer in its place.*

I was nineteen years old when he gave me the cassette. Apart from my father and brother, no male – boy or man – had seen me since I turned eight. Father had bought me a long black coat, a *baltu*, that covered my body from neck to foot, and a headscarf and veil with two small slits for the eyes. I was thrilled when I saw myself in the mirror: I had become a woman, like Mother.

By the time I was twelve years old, however, I wanted my father to stop buying me *baltus* and let me wear the black cloak-like abaya instead, like the one I'd seen at my niece's wedding. The girl I heard them call Adaniya wore an abaya wrapped round her shoulders and open at the front. It revealed her body so clearly it was almost as though she were naked. In fact, she would have been less alluring without the abaya on at all.

For months I dreamt of wearing an abaya, but eventually I became convinced I'd never own one.

I was happy with the *baltu* and the veil when I was eight, but by the age of twelve all I wanted was an abaya. When finally Father announced he was going to buy me one, I thought it would be like Adaniya's. I had no idea it would be so different until he brought it home, complete with headscarf and veil. Mother explained to me that what we were used to calling the *baltu* – my mother, sister and I all wore one – was also known as the abaya, and that the style of abaya worn by Adaniya was called something different altogether.

That day, I felt weighed down for the first time. I no longer walked but rolled along, a black blob. Standing in front of the mirror, I asked myself: What's the point of this body of mine?

I hadn't yet realised that others didn't see me as bearing

a burden; for them I was the burden myself, a burden whose presence continually bothered them.

> *In my chest there is only flesh and blood*
> *Feeble now that youth has gone.*

I don't know: have I lived my youth as I should have done? Have I even lived at all? Honestly, I don't even know what youth means – is it the years that pass us by during a certain period of our lives or is it how we live during those years?

I don't have the answer.

For years I couldn't even ask a question. If I thought there was a question in a sentence, I was unable to indicate it with a question mark. Why did my teacher beat me for drawing a heart? That was the first question I asked. And why did Father beat me so hard?

When he heard me asking Mother that in the living room, he stormed out of the bathroom and gave me another beating. He slapped me on the cheeks, and all over my head, yelling, 'After everything you've learned you still ask why!'

> *Even if hearts were made of iron*
> *Still none could bear what mine has suffered.*

I was in my fourth year of primary school when it happened. Before the Islamic education teacher arrived for class, my friend pulled a piece of paper from her bag. It was decorated with roses, and in the middle was what she described as a heart pierced by an arrow. Her big sister had drawn it to give to the boy next door – she'd written her name on the heart, and his on the arrow. My friend whispered to me that her sister didn't know she'd taken it. She let out a loud peal of laughter, obviously intended to arouse the curiosity of our classmates. Everyone looked at us, including the teacher who'd just entered the classroom.

'What's going on?' she bellowed as my friend stuffed the piece of paper back into her bag.

'Nothing Miss, nothing,' we both said at the same time.

Even if hearts were made of iron

Yes, Miss Om Kalthoum, even if. I, however, made a heart from paper and ink.

I was baffled by my classmate's fascination with her sister's drawing. I didn't understand her embarrassment or why she hid it away so quickly. Her whispering and giggling had stirred something inside me, making it impossible to concentrate on the lesson. I'm not sure why I tore a page from my exercise book and tried to draw the heart and arrow from memory. I don't know what happened, but when I came around I found myself in the headmistress's office, my head, chest and back sopping wet. The headmistress was standing beside the Islamic Education teacher, telling her: 'Not like that, Miss. I've told you more than once to hit them on the hand, not the head.' I felt my head and realised she was talking about me. It seemed the teacher had hit me on the head and knocked me out, and I'd only come to after they'd poured water over me.

'Bring your children up properly!' the headmistress told my father, having called him into the school. 'This one has no shame. Drawing hearts, writing love letters, idle gossiping.'

My father certainly got the message. That day, I learnt that 'bring up properly' meant 'beat.' But I still didn't know what drawing hearts meant, or what the headmistress had meant about love letters and idle gossip.

I wasn't allowed to ask. From that day on and for many years afterwards I was no longer able to ask questions, or to even include a question mark in any of my assignments. In fact, I couldn't so much as think about using one. Perhaps during those years I forgot what a question mark was. At the end of any uncertain phrase or sentence I would simply put a full stop to mute its uncertainty. Or I'd add a second full stop to silence it completely.

When was it that I finally remembered the existence of question marks? Whenever it was, I began to add them to the end of every single line, whether one was needed or not.

> *No one can tell you about life's hardships*
> *Like someone who has lost their loved ones can.*

Once, there were boys in my life: cousins, uncles, the neighbours' children. They were my friends and loved ones. When I turned eight they disappeared as though they'd never existed. I am a girl, therefore I should not talk about them, or even mention their names. 'Careful, my girl. It's a sin.'

I really wanted Mother to explain to me why it was a sin. I figured that stating this desire would be just that, a statement. But then I thought again and decided against it. I reasoned that the desire to understand was in fact a type of question, and I had no right to be asking questions.

Nashwan, who lived close by, was around the same age

as me. He was really good at making paper kites. Every child in the neighbourhood had a kite, but Nashwan's was still the best. It could fly further and higher than all the others. He would chase after it, clutching the string, as the kite flew higher and higher. He flew his kite like an ace pilot. I never imagined that the kite would slip from his grasp one day.

The last time we met he had the string wrapped around all ten of his fingers. Leaping and whooping, he raised his hands above his head and spread his fingers, letting the string unspool completely until he freed the very end of the string. I watched the kite as it floated off.

'Why did you let it fly away from you?' I asked Nashwan.

'It hasn't, I'm flying with it,' he said.

I wanted to ask him why he didn't take me with him, but it was too late; Nashwan had already floated far, far away from me.

Side B of the Om Kalthoum tape

When I was in my first year of secondary school I learned why my brother, Raqeeb, liked to call me Ruza. One day he gave me a book called *Love Letters*. When I read the title, the headmistress' accusing words from three years earlier came back to me.

No one in the house called me by my name. Mother called me 'Little Mama' to distinguish between me and Lula, my older sister, whom she affectionately called 'Mummy.' I think perhaps she called her this to compensate for losing her own mother at a young age. Whenever I heard my father calling 'Girl! Where's the girl?' I knew that he meant me. Lula called me 'Pipsqueak' and never ceased to find it amusing. That was the name I liked best, to the extent that if anyone asked me my name I would almost answer 'Pipsqueak!'

But my brother used to call me Ruza. 'Be free and wonderful like Rosa Luxemburg!' he would say, 'Read her book and you'll learn what really matters in life.'

Love Letters was the first book Raqeeb gave me to read behind our father's back.

I didn't really understand when my brother said to Lula,

'I'm telling you, in the end socialism will prevail.' Lula didn't even try to hide her cynicism, telling Raqeeb that he was behind the times. 'You're completely deluded! Don't you know the Soviet Union collapsed ages ago?'

His message was a path to the light
His horses rode forth in the cause of right.

What does Om Kalthoum's song mean?

We didn't have a stereo or a television at home. There was just my father's old Russian radio. And day in, day out, he only ever listened to the same two stations.

'It's either the BBC Arabic Service or Holy Quran Radio from the honoured city of Mecca. What a joke. The irony of a radio made in the land of the Bolsheviks, the land of the great Vladimir Lenin, being only used to receive the transmissions of an imperialist state or a reactionary one.'

Raqeeb would often say this kind of thing, but of course never in front of Father. Father would lock the radio away in a trunk whenever he left the house, along with the phone. If Mother ran out of something in the kitchen she'd have to wait until he got home before she could call the neighbour, Suhail's mum, or Umm Nura – 'Nura's mum' – as she was also known. Umm Nura would get one of her children to pass us what Mother needed through the door: an onion, a head of garlic, some salt or sugar.

It seemed Mother wasn't allowed to call out to her neighbour from the window. I only discovered why this was much later, when the Islamic Education teacher told us: 'A women's voice is as private as her face, and should not be heard in public, just like her face should not be seen.'

Lula had the latest mobile phone, but I was the only one in the house who knew about it.

One day, when I was in my third year of secondary school, a classmate slipped a videocassette into my bag. 'We don't have a video player at home, or a television,' I said. The next day, she whispered 'Did you like the cultural film? I know you won't want to give it back.' I didn't reply. I just smiled and shook my head as if to say I definitely would be.

Back at home, I said to Lula 'A friend gave me a cultural video, but I don't know how I'm supposed to watch it.' She looked at me, horrified, and pulled me into the kitchen by my arm.

'What? What? What did you just say, Pipsqueak? Be careful no one hears you! Are you trying to drive me out of my mind, Pipsqueak?'

I didn't understand what all the fuss was about. Then she added, in an angry whisper, 'Father's forbidden us from watching television because he doesn't want us to see men on it, and you want to watch a cultural film in the house?' She continued, her voice still rising, 'Father said that seeing men on TV and hearing their voices is the same as being alone with them and is forbidden by God's law and you . . . you . . .'

'What should I do, Lula? My friend asked me if I'd watched the film and if I liked it. What am I going to tell her? Do you think I should I give it back?'

'Are you sure it's a cultural film?' she asked. Then, without waiting for an answer, she decided: 'Tell her you saw it and that it was good. It's like any cultural film – zeet-meet.'

I shook my head, puzzled.

'Don't you know what zeet-meet is? You know –
sucking, licking, fucking. A man on top of a woman,
mounting her. Or a woman crouching over a man and
moving up and down on him.'

'Uhhh . . . What? What are you saying? That's what
cultural films are?'

She looked at me, and realised I had no idea what she
was talking about.

'Pipsqueak, after everything I've just said you still don't
get it?'

She chuckled, and added, 'Give her back her video and
as soon as I get the chance I'll take you to my friend's
house, where you can watch a cultural film and learn what
zeet-meet is for yourself.'

He taught us how to gain glory
So that we took command of the land by force.

My classmate stopped asking me about the video and I
didn't attempt to return it. I kept it hidden between my
exercise books so that it was always with me as I travelled
to and from school. I hoped she wouldn't ask again, at least
not before I'd been able to watch it. The chance to watch
the video seemed like the chance of a lifetime, one I just
couldn't afford to miss. I had the feeling that most of my
classmates had already had that chance, or many chances, in
fact. I guess it was obvious from the way they walked – sexy,
seductive – so different to me.

In the morning, straight after registration, or at the end of
lunch before the teacher arrived for class, the girls would
take it in turns to show off their moves. One girl would start
it off, swaying her hips as she stepped into the classroom,

gyrating her whole body like the dancer I'd seen once in an Egyptian movie. She'd slink between the desks and chairs until she reached the back of the classroom, and then sit down in her usual seat for another girl to take over and strut her stuff.

At first I was terrible at it, but I refused to give up. Every day, I tried to imitate their movements, until eventually the other girls stopped laughing at me. In fact, I got so good their derision turned into something approaching admiration. There were two girls who stayed outside the flock, refusing to even spectate. We called one of them 'Sheikh' – like an elder, or a religious authority – and the other 'Mujahid' – as in one of the mujahideen. As soon as they set foot in the classroom, the other girls would all shout 'Sheikh Mujahid has arrived!' as though they were one person. But I never joined in. After a few days of this, Sheikh and Mujahid took to waiting until after the teacher had arrived before taking their seats. The girls' jeers were replaced with barely suppressed laughter.

> Demands are not met by wishing
> The world can only be won through struggle.

As he opened the front door on his way to work in the morning, we would always hear Father recite 'O Fattah, O 'Aleem, O Razzaq, O Kareem!' This was the one prayer that would really wind Raqeeb up. Every time he heard Father reciting it, he'd mutter, 'If God truly existed then He would provide for you and make you a rich man – not out of mercy, but because He's so bored and fed up with listening to your prayers.' Mother would angrily yell at him 'God save your soul! Don't you blaspheme! Have you forgotten who created you?' I used to wonder what Father would do if he ever overheard Raqeeb's comments.

Once, as Father was leaving the house, reciting 'He provides for whosoever he wishes without account. There is no God but God,' Raqeeb burst out laughing. 'That's totally whimsical. He makes rich whoever He wants, and makes poor whoever He wants. How can anyone worship a God who behaves like that?' When she heard this Mother completely lost it. She screamed and screamed at him, calling him a blasphemer, and asking God to punish her son for his bad words. Raqeeb's hysterical laughter drowned out the sound of Mother's sobbing. No one could stop him − except Nura, the neighbours' daughter, who came over to see Lula later that afternoon.

The three of us were sitting together − Lula, Nura and I − when Mother, holding back her tears, came in and said she would make tea for the guest. Lula turned to Nura, who was a close friend of hers, and said, in a mock-theatrical tone, 'This is our duty, O dear guest. We must honour you.' Lula and I began to laugh so loudly that Raqeeb burst into the room, eager to know what we'd found so funny. On catching sight of Nura he stopped still, frozen in embarrassment. 'Sorry . . .' he said, his eyes glued to Nura, 'I didn't realise you had someone with you.' He seemed transfixed, unable to speak or move. He only left the room after Nura ducked down behind us, hunching over to conceal her body's curves, which she'd freed from her abaya when she entered the house. The absurdity of the situation made us laugh even harder. Nura did an impression of Raqeeb, who she said had stormed into the room like a policeman catching a criminal red-handed. Lula thought he'd looked more like the husband who bursts in on his wife to find her in the arms of another man. But neither of their comparisons rang true to me. He hadn't reacted predictably, like the policeman or the husband would. Instead he'd become embarrassed, stammered and left the room in a way that called more for sympathy and even astonishment than it did laughter.

'I want to marry that girl. Please, ask her family for her hand,' Raqeeb said to Mother as soon as Nura left. We hadn't realised he'd been that smitten by her.

The Philosopher, as Father used to call my brother, had refused every one of Mother's many attempts to marry him to the daughters of her relatives or friends. He would say he wanted an open-minded girl who didn't wear an abaya or even a headscarf, and who was free – both of the reactionaries' legacy and of the greedy ways of the capitalists. I wondered if he'd found these things in Nura, a girl he'd never seen before. I don't think he'd set eyes on her without her abaya, headscarf and veil since she was ten or younger – even if their front door was directly opposite ours, just a few steps away.

Mother, taken aback by his sudden request, tried to dissuade him.

'There are better and prettier girls out there.'

'There aren't any better or prettier than Nura.'

'The daughters of God are many, my son.'

'He has not, nor will He, ever create another like Nura.'

It was the first time I'd heard Raqeeb acknowledge the existence of God as our creator, even if indirectly. He had always insisted that we call him just Raqeeb, instead of by his full name 'Abd al-Raqeeb, meaning Servant of the Watchful One. He insisted that he didn't recognise himself as a servant of 'the Watchful One' – one of God's ninety-nine names. How was it possible that the very person who had encouraged me to study the principles of Georges Politzer's philosophy, to struggle through a condensed volume of Lenin's writings on the school of empirical criticism, could so easily switch creeds?

> *Nothing is beyond the reach of a people*
> *When their feet are firmly in the stirrups.*

Once our mother had secured Nura's hand for her only son, all that was left was to wait for the wedding day. Raqeeb was nine years older than me, and Lula six years. Despite having got his baccalaureate in English literature two years earlier, Raqeeb still hadn't found a job. Lula, on the other hand, started working for an import and export company as soon as she finished secondary school. Begrudgingly, Father also agreed to her attending university, so she had to balance work and study. Lula would leave the house early in the morning and not return until late in the evening. The monthly contribution she gave Father from her salary was sufficiently generous for him to turn a blind eye and not scrutinise her comings and goings like he did mine.

Once a week Father would work the night shift. It was on one such night, while he was busy refuelling electricity generators, that Lula gave me my first dose of culture.

A Cultural Cassette Tape

'It's zeet-meet time!' said Lula, locking the bedroom door. She produced a cassette from her handbag and inserted into a little tape player she'd borrowed from one of her workmates, and we got comfortable and started listening to it. It's on this same cassette player – which remained hidden away among Lula's personal things and never made it back to its owner – that I'm listening to all these old tapes again right now.

'Oh . . . Oh . . . Ah . . . Ah . . . Please, stick it in . . . Fuck me, please. Fuck me . . . Put the head in.'

It was a surprise to hear such things being said – actually, the biggest surprise of my life so far. It was a day I'd never forget. I was confused, and almost asked Lula: 'What's the woman on the tape saying? What does she mean? Who's she talking to?' But soon enough my body began to work out the answers for itself, and showed me, from head to toe, that it knew exactly what was going on. In that moment, my body seemed more consumed by what it felt than I was myself. For a second, I felt as though I were outside my body, separate from it. Then I realised – perhaps I'd been lost in the moment – that I wasn't outside it, but under its control. It dominated all my senses, my every thought, word and movement, revealing the hidden things in what I was hearing and encouraging me to listen more closely.

'Please. Just the head . . . Please . . . Yes . . . Yes like that. Yes . . . Yes . . . Push it in, please. Please . . . Push it in, please . . . Please . . . Please . . . Please . . . Please . . .'

I was entranced by the sound, and by the strong Egyptian accent. I've no idea how many times I heard the word 'please.' Lula turned down the volume, but the words that came from the cassette player didn't seem to grow any quieter. Instead, they sounded louder and louder. I felt as though the words were coming from my body, and not the anonymous voice on the cassette.

★

'Yes . . . Yes . . . Like that . . .'

'How is it?' A man's voice asks.

'It's nice.'

'What's nice?'

'Your thing . . . your thing is lovely. Sweeter than honey.'

'My what?'

'Your thing . . . your cock . . . your cock . . . Please, just let it slide in. Put it inside me.'

We moved our heads closer to the cassette player until our ears were pressed right up against the little speaker.

'We agreed, just the head,' he tells her.

'For me . . . Please . . . For my pussy . . . Put half of it in . . . Yes . . . Yes . . . A little more. Put it in a little more . . . Halfway in . . . Please, half of it . . . It's so nice . . . Yeah . . . Yeah . . . Like that . . . Yes . . . Sweet . . . Sweet . . .'

'What's sweet?'

'Your cock . . . Your sweet cock . . . Yes . . . Yes . . . That's nice . . . Yes . . . Yes . . . Yes . . . Yes . . . Yes . . . Fuck me hard. Put it in . . . Please, all of it . . . All of it . . . All, all . . . Ah . . . Ahhhh.'

At this point Lula paused the tape. She said she'd heard something outside the door. I froze. My muscles tensed and my body cried out in protest. I begged her to let the tape finish.

'That's enough. It's all the same thing.'

'I just want to know what happens at the end. Please.'

'What do you think happens at the end?!'

'Does he put it all in? And what do they do after that?'

'Oh dear! We've let her watch through the keyhole and now she wants to come in!' She said, laughing.

★

I didn't sleep that night, or the next. Perhaps I've never really had a good night's sleep again since then.

The next night we listened to the cassette again. Lula had kept it hidden among her secret things. This time we were more cautious. Father was at home, and he was a very light sleeper who woke often during the night.

I noticed the cassette label, written by hand, said 'Local Sex.' Lula and I huddled together, listening to the same words, the same moans and groans. The pleasure I felt became so much more intense when I wrapped my thighs around Lula's leg. I was burning up, trembling. She reached out her right hand and pulled my knickers down to my knees, stroking my thighs, and then gradually moving her hands in between them. She turned me over onto my back, put her index finger on my clitoris and rubbed it vigorously. At first I laughed because it tickled. She whispered for me to be quiet and then began to alternately rub around and my clitoris and right on it. The tape played on: 'Put it all in . . . Yes . . . Please . . . Put it in . . . Put it in.' I was on fire, writhing against her touch until I almost screamed out.

It took me a while to calm down. Didn't Lula need my finger too? I reached for her crotch, but she pushed my hand away, saying 'I'm like the woman on the cassette. I want him – zeet-meet. I want him to put the whole thing all the way in. I want him to fuck me, to pound me again and again until I'm satisfied. Until he kills me, and leaves me dead.'

I was shocked by what I heard. Wasn't she still a virgin? Had she lost her virginity, which our mother had told us a hundred times to keep intact at all costs? She'd even made us scared of jumping up and down because it might cause us to lose our virginity – our honour and the family's honour, as she used to put it.

A few months earlier, I'd felt the wetness of that dark liquid between my thighs for the first time, and rushed to Mother. 'Don't be scared, you've matured! You've become a woman, my girl.'

Had I become a woman without knowing who my man would be – the man I'd writhe beneath like the woman on the tape? Was she on top, or was he on top of her? Perhaps he was beneath her, while she reached for him, struggling with him as he gripped his thing, only giving it to her in small, delicious doses, bit by bit until it was all the way in.

Side B of the Om Kalthoum tape (replay)

Raqeeb didn't actually oppose Nura continuing her university studies, but he bombarded her with questions about her lecture times, professors and classmates. He quizzed her on their names and what they looked like, including the way they dressed and even their hairstyles. He'd also want to know who she'd talked to during the day.

Nura turned out to be cunning in a way I never would have expected. I was sitting next to her when she said to Raqeeb: 'Imagine, there was this really good-looking guy, the sort who likes to take care of himself. I think he wanted to talk to me. He said "Good morning," but I ignored him. I kept on walking but he followed me and said, "Please, can you let me see your notes for psychology? I missed the lecture."'

Raqeeb's face was tense with anxiety as she spoke, until she came to the part of the story when she said, 'But I carried on walking. I didn't look back, or even say a word to him.' As soon as he heard this Raqeeb's face relaxed and he looked happy again.

Mother sold her gold to pay a quarter of Nura's dowry, while Lula pulled together another quarter. We were all intrigued as to how Raqeeb was able to provide the remaining half, since he'd only started working the day after he first saw Nura and decided he wanted to marry her.

Raqeeb stopped reading into the early hours. He now had to get up early for his new teaching job at an English language school. It was as if he'd swapped reading for Nura. In the weeks leading up to the wedding, whenever I asked him what he was thinking about he'd tell me he was thinking about her and their future together. After the wedding, however, it was clearly his passion for her hot body that occupied his nights, if not every single minute of his life.

His message was . . .

I haven't really paid much attention to the first verse of the song. I'll listen to it again later, when I'm not so preoccupied.

The biggest change at home wasn't Nura's arrival, it was Raqeeb's newfound commitment to the five daily prayers. This, of course, included the dawn prayer. The first time he came into our room to wake us up for the dawn prayer we thought he was joking: 'Come, let's punish the Devil and pray. God will make you happy and provide you with upright and respectable offspring.'

'What – What did you say? Say it again.' Lula managed to sound sarcastic even when still half asleep.

'It's best if you get up. Prayer is better than sleep!' He answered her.

It was my turn: 'What a convincing performance, our

dear master, our Sheikh. Go back to your wife's side and let us sleep.' But he was serious, and wouldn't leave us alone until we'd got up to pray. There was no use in arguing, especially since we could hear Father moving around, having also risen to pray.

'A dangerous religious deviation,' said Lula as she got back into bed after praying. She burst out laughing, pulling the blankets up over her head to try and muffle the sound. We whispered together about this sudden change in Raqeeb until neither of us were able to get back to sleep. Out of all of us, Raqeeb had been the one who never prayed unless he was forced to – and even then he did so without any real conviction. In those days I'd just go through the motions. I'd make my ablutions in the bathroom, and then disappear into the bedroom for a while, and Mother and Father would assume I was deep in prayer. Lula saw prayer as a sort of exercise which she'd practice from time to time. She might sometimes sleep in a little and be late in starting the dawn prayer, but she always managed to finish before the sun had fully risen.

Later that morning, Lula took Nura by the hand and pulled her into our room. 'What's with you? What have you done to Raqeeb? Instead of taming him you've led him astray!'

'What do mean?' asked Nura.

'Our master, the great Sheikh Raqeeb, the authority on Marx, Lenin, and our grandmother Rosa Luxemburg, on the material world, and idealism – this same man now wants to drag us all out of bed at the crack of dawn as soon as the call to prayer sounds.'

'I've done this? He's asked me to start wearing the abaya, to be more "modest." He said to me "What's the use of studying psychology?" I'm afraid he's going to tell me to quit.'

'Tame him, show him the joys of life. Feed him! What are you doing?'

'Your brother's backward. Tribal. Who brought him up to be like that?' said Nura, laughing.

He taught us how to gain glory
So that we took command of the land by force.

I was expecting my friend to ask me about the videocassette, but to my surprise she brought me another. At first, I assumed it was a gift. I suggested we could go with Nura to her parents' house to watch the two films. Lula arranged it with Nura, although she wasn't too happy to find I still had the first tape.

Two Cultural Videos

I'm going to play the films on Lula's mobile phone. She used it to record the films as we watched them that day – she was very keen on making her own copies.

Two naked bodies. A man and woman. Licking and sucking. Groans and moans. Opening and entering. Zeet-meet. The bodies entwined, face to face in a sitting position. Then he lies on his back and she climbs on top of him like a horse-rider mounting her steed. She rides him and rides him, all the way.

The second film was more like a guide to sexual intercourse. With each new scenario, Lula would say the same thing to Nura – 'Look and learn. Let him do the work and feed you the zeet-meet. Taste the pleasures of life.'

Nura would just laugh. It was obvious she'd seen films like it before, although she lacked Lula's practical experience.

One of the scenes really caught my imagination: I wanted to do it just like that.

A woman is sleeping in her bed. A man comes into the room and undresses, then pulls the bedcovers off her. Her body is clearly visible through her flimsy nightie. He slips his hand under the nightie and strokes her neck and breasts. The insistent, circular movement of his hand arouses her. He does this for a few minutes before moving down to her waist, making the same circular motions. He moves further down, between her thighs, under her knickers, which he effortlessly removes. The woman looks like she's still asleep, unaware of what's happening to her body. He opens her legs and begins to kiss between her thighs. He pulls her greedily towards his mouth, his nose, his whole face. The camera zooms in on him gently kissing her pussy . . . A second, third and forth kiss. His lips touch her clitoris. He kisses it and teases it with the tip of his tongue. He moves his tongue faster, licking and sucking on her clitoris [Ooohhh I shouldn't be watching this again]. His tongue flicks in all directions – up, down, round and round, licking her pussy all over. She's clearly no longer able to hide her excitement, even though she pretends she's still sleeping.

He straightens up on his knees and then presses himself into her and the zeet-meet begins.

Some time passes while he thrusts and pounds, without the camera showing us any details. When he's finished the man carefully puts her panties back on and replaces the bedcovers before leaving.

The woman wakes up feeling aroused. She looks around her, as if wondering 'Was I dreaming, or did that really happen?'

Let me return to Om Kalthoum . . .

Demands are not met by wishing
The world can only be won through struggle.

'Abd al-Raqeeb, who now refused to be called merely Raqeeb, filled the house with religious recordings and books. He made a fire on the roof area outside his room and burned all the revolutionary pamphlets and cassettes he'd collected during his 'wayward years,' as he now referred to that period of his life.

On his first day as a married man, 'Abd al-Raqeeb chose the room next to ours for him and his new bride. We rearranged the room, and redistributed the things that had been stored in it around the house, but in the end they only spent four nights in it. Nura said he didn't want us to hear their nightly antics. He preferred them to sleep in the room on the roof, far away from us.

'Does Sheikh 'Abd al-Raqeeb even know what fun and laughter are anymore?' asked Lula. As usual, Nura gave a little giggle.

Nothing is beyond the reach of a people
When their feet are firmly in the stirrups.

When Suhail gave me the Om Kalthoum cassette, I'd already decided to study at the Islamic University once I finished school. It was a popular option, especially since the only acceptance condition was to memorise three of the Noble

Quran's thirty sections and be able to recite them correctly – and according to what I'd heard from other girls who'd studied there, the recitation wasn't strictly necessary. Up until a few years earlier we hadn't even heard of the Islamic University. It would have been so much easier if I'd only had to memorise three parts of the Quran, and not spend three years at the Islamic Scientific Academy. Those years passed by as though I'd never really lived them. I wanted to complete my secondary education at the same school I'd attended for nine years. I wanted to stay with my friends, but this wasn't to be. One day when we were eating dinner, 'Abd al-Raqeeb said, 'Tomorrow morning, go and register at the Islamic Scientific Academy. The one close to here – it's just a couple of streets down. I'll drop you off in front of it. The religious science academies are much better than the schools, they teach their pupils according to the true Islamic way.'

As soon as he said this, my father looked over at me. 'Did you hear what your brother said? You'll go with him tomorrow.' I didn't have a say in the matter.

Nothing is beyond the reach of a people

From day one I sensed the Academy was going to be completely different from my old school. In the morning, as I passed through the main gate, I noticed a woman standing beside the door holding a long cane. She placed her left hand on my right shoulder and looked me up and down, scrutinising my clothing. Then, abruptly, she whipped her cane up in the air.

'What's this joke? Have you come here to study, or to

dance?' I didn't know what to say. She pointed to the gate with her cane.

'Go home. Now. Don't come back until you've put on a loose abaya and covered your face with a real veil, not that flimsy thing you're wearing. And buy a pair of flat-heeled, Islamic shoes.'

When I got home, Lula hadn't yet left the house. She rummaged through her wardrobe and pulled out an old abaya, saying, 'Perhaps this one will do?' She returned to the pile of clothes to find a veil, adding, 'What more could they want? You look like a tent. No one's going to be able to see you dressed like that.'

I needed to get back to the Academy. On the way out of the door, the world looked different: it was darker. After I put on the thick veil the sky looked like a big shadow, consuming the earth and stretching into the horizon. Everything around me had become one big shadow, the shadow cast by an invisible light.

I remembered the 'Islamic shoes' and went back to Lula.

'The shoes you're wearing are already as low as they get.'

'Perhaps a few extra millimetres are all it takes to be in violation of sharia?' I said to her.

'Enough! Talk to your brother, the sheikh, it's his duty to buy you a pair of shoes that meet sharia standards.' This time she seemed angry. I quickly slipped my shoes back on and left.

Abu al-Zahra, I've overstepped my rank
In praising you, yet I seek the honour.

At the academy I learned that 'Abu al-Zahra' is one of the names given to the Prophet, Muhammad, after his daughter,

Fatima al-Zahra. Om Kalthoum's song praises a beloved with the same name. Why did Suhail give me this particular song?

Life at the Academy was always serious. No one ever dared joke or laugh, except for Leena. It was as if she had been born from a joke, or that she had grown up in a house of laughter. As soon as the teacher left the classroom, Leena would raise her voice to address our classmate, Nahla, who'd been chosen as the class president.

'O Sheikha Nahla, am I permitted to tell you all a joke?' The first time, Nahla was silent for a moment, before replying, 'It is permitted. It is permitted, but only on condition that it is told in an Islamic way.'

The girls burst into laughter at such a serious answer. This became a running joke. Leena would tease Nahla by asking her the same question. When she refused to reply, some of the other students would answer for her, so that as soon as Leena opened her mouth and began to ask 'Is it permitted to—' they would raise their voices and drown her out with a chorus of 'It is permitted. It is permitted, but . . .'

Within these limitations we would laugh. Leena didn't even need to tell a joke; she'd just ask her usual question and we'd all be laughing.

One time Leena cut across our laughter, with 'Do you know what I was going to ask before you all started saying It is permitted, it is permitted?'

We all fell silent, sensing there was something behind her words.

'If any of you are rude, I'll write your name on the board for teacher to see,' Nahla would always threaten. She only ever carried out her threat once, when she complained to the Quran teacher that the students kept

laughing and joking. 'If that's the case, then firstly, they
wanted to tell a joke, and secondly, they were going to
laugh when they heard it,' said the teacher, trying to work
out the appropriate judgement to be passed on those who
had dared not only to tell a joke but to laugh at it, too. But
just at that moment, one of the Academy's Administrators
came along. She told the teacher that her family had been
in touch and had asked that she come home straightaway,
as her mother was sick. She shrieked, rushing from the
classroom as though her mother was already dead.

I have praised kings and risen high in their esteem
But when I praise you I rise above the clouds.

I stopped just going through the motions of prayer and
began to pray in earnest. At first I missed my old school:
lining up for morning registration, then standing to attention as the national anthem played, until it accompanied
our measured steps from the playground to class. I also
missed the sports. But I quickly learned that what I missed
was in violation of sharia.

'This is the way of the new age of ignorance, it violates
sharia – God's law – completely, in spirit and in letter . . .'
I heard this sort of thing often in relation to all and every
aspect of life. A fatwa, or religious ruling, was always to
hand, hemming me in on all sides. Fatwas were cited in
answer to any question, spoken or unspoken: Is it OK for
a woman to go outside without a male guardian, related
to her through birth or marriage? Is it wrong to walk too
slow or too fast? It is OK to read novels and magazines?
Most of the rulings dealt with issues that were embarrassing
for someone of my age: What was the appropriate ruling

for a woman handling cucumbers and bananas, cooking with squash and aubergine, sleeping naked, talking to men, shaking a man's hand, embracing another woman, being taken by her husband from behind, seeing dogs or chickens copulate. A fatwa was required for everything, and for every conceivable situation in life it would be asked 'Is this, according to sharia, permitted or prohibited?' Even crying and laughing. I considered laughter within the bounds of sharia but I couldn't work out whether I was free to cry. I searched and searched in books for a legal pretext that would give me the right to cry, however and whenever I liked. I spent days and months researching and comparing various opinions. Eventually, my own independent judgement, or 'ijtihad' as it's known in sharia, led me to conclude I had the right to cry. But when I wanted to cry, I found I'd forgotten how to.

Three years passed during which I felt I was in an endless state of jihad, a religious warrior battling the everyday. I became obsessed with the great Islamic issues: jihad in Afghanistan and Chechnya against the heathen crusaders and the communists, fighting the Jews in Palestine, and infidels in general, wherever they might be.

By my final year at the Academy, my relationship with Lula had changed. Once while I prayed she heard me asking God to give me the good fortune to go to Afghanistan or Palestine to do jihad and become a martyr.

'What? Jihad? Live a little first! Zeet-meet, that's jihad,' she said before I'd even finished my prayer.

'What are you saying? You're disobeying God. Why are you being so blasphemous?'

'When have I ever disobeyed God? What is there for God to dislike if we're enjoying our lives?'

'We should only enjoy what is halal, what is permitted.'

'Halal, halal. Let a man mount you with his halal. After that, you won't want to run after jihad or anything else. You'll want to martyr yourself beneath him, taking his thrusts.'

She started laughing and wouldn't stop, even though she could see I was angry: 'Instead of allowing yourself to be martyred by the thrusts of an infidel in Afghanistan or Chechnya or Palestine, martyr yourself here. Go and pick a fight with any old infidel and let him stab you to death.'

Lula had just got back from a trip to London, but unusually for her, she hadn't told me anything about it yet.

She'd started testing the waters, to try and gauge how I'd react before telling me about her sexual adventures and how much she loved Europe.

I remember how she'd gone on about her trip to Germany for months, all starry-eyed:

'There are people there. People. Not like the people here.'

'Why did you come back then? You could have stayed there.'

'What would I do? There are more than enough whores over there.'

'Couldn't you find any other work apart from that?'

'You know that's my preferred line of work.'

The truth is, Lula wasn't really a whore, exactly. Her activities were limited, and she rarely had relations with anyone other than her boss. Even so, this is how she liked to describe herself.

After her trip to Norway we had pretty much the same conversation, but her trip to Paris was like nothing else. Her life was turned completely upside down, a life she'd begun too early.

★

A few months before I enrolled at the Islamic Scientific Academy, Lula wanted to show me where she worked. She'd told me she worked for an import and export business. When we arrived there were three girls sitting at neighbouring desks. They chattered amongst themselves, their conversation eliciting a near constant stream of laughter. Lula quickly led me into another room.

'What's the matter with you? Come and sit down and introduce us to your sis!' said one of them.

'I don't want you corrupting her with your loose morals!' replied Lula, laughing.

'Loose morals! It's bad enough she lives with you, isn't it? Or do you never go home?' They laughed some more.

'Aren't there any men working here?' I asked her.

'Of course there are. There's the boss. Then there's the accountant who works here one day a week. And there's also a man who comes in every afternoon around two o'clock. He deals with foreign transactions, business relations, stuff like that.'

'What about the girls, what do they do?'

'As you can see, sometimes we print documents and letters. One translates letters into English, the other is the office secretary – she records all the imports and exports and prepares the paperwork for the accountant. She's also the one who opens and closes the office. The other is a butterfly who just flutters around looking pretty. Sometimes she cleans the office and makes tea and coffee for the boss.'

'And what do you do?'

'I'm still in training. I've only been here eight months.'

She answered the phone on her desk. 'OK. I'm coming. OK!' She repeated this several times, giggling.

After she hung up she said: 'I also answer the phone

for the boss – but only for the boss. He has two lines, one in his office and one in here with me. Didn't I tell you? I'm training to become his PA. His last one went for the office secretary position.'

Lula dropped me back home. She said it was the boss who'd called. He'd asked her to return to work later that day, to fill in for someone.

'All of us have to pull an afternoon shift, ten consecutive days a month. Ha, if only you could see the work that's done in the afternoon! The boss keeps me busy in ways you couldn't imagine.'

'God protect you.'

'No, it's not hard work. It's lovely, delicious work.'

Lula was really into buying these transparent, risqué nighties. She kept them stashed away with her perfumes in a locked suitcase. Father was always very happy when she gave him a chunk of her salary, so he went along with everything 'Abd al-Raqeeb said, except stopping Lula from working or travelling. Later, she told me all about the extra work she did in the afternoon: 'The boss doesn't make me work in the afternoon, except for the ten days before the start of my period.'

'You said the five days after the period are safe, and that a woman can't get pregnant during this time if she—'

'True, true,' Lula cut me off, 'but there are ten safe days if you count from the first day of the period. But the boss likes to work during the ten days before my period. I like this time too because I'm hornier before it than I am after.'

'What? You like it?'

'Yep. Understand?'

'And he works with the rest of the girls like this?'

'No! He swears it's just me. The others come into the office as and when their work requires it.'

'And what do they say?'

'They don't know and I don't tell them anything. The only things we do together are watch cultural films and the afternoon prayer.'

'I know what the cultural films are, but what's going on with the afternoon prayer?'

'According to the boss's instructions, five minutes before the call to prayer we play a cassette of the Quran, recited by Abdulbasit Abdulsamad, the Egyptian Quran reciter, and turn up the volume so that everyone in the building can hear. When we hear the call to prayer from the three nearby mosques blaring out we roll out the prayer rug in the office lounge and pray behind Samira, who leads the prayer.'

'And if Samira doesn't lead the prayer, do you do it?'

She let out a long laugh and then said: 'Yeah right, me an imam! You mean if she's on her period? No, it's not a problem. It's all just for show anyway, for the owner of the building, the boss's father-in-law. He's really religious.'

'I don't understand. What's the point, even if it's all just for show?'

'Oh Pipsqueak. The owner of the building is rich and it looks good for the boss. If he sees us praying like that then he won't worry about us trying to seduce his daughter's husband and corrupt him, because we're righteous women who say all our prayers.'

'But what if he's the one doing the seducing?'

'They say woman is a devil who seduces man – that if it wasn't for her he'd remain pure.'

★

Not too long after I visited the office, Lula's boss decided to close the business. He opened up a new office as part of some international campaign to save endangered species. The nature of his work meant that he was often out of the country. Not a month would go by without him having to travel – usually at least twice – to take part in some conference or workshop. He took Lula on three trips: to New York, Berlin and London. She told me that as soon as they got through the door of their hotel room, he'd start pestering her to swap the heavy layers that concealed her figure for clothes that showed it off. But then, once she was dressed as requested, more provocatively, he wouldn't allow her to leave the room. So she would stay there until it was time to pack their suitcases and leave.

'When he finally agreed to let me represent the organisation at the special session on animal rights in Paris, I was freer than I ever was when I travelled with him. A whole month of freedom! As soon as I boarded the plane I went into the toilet and changed my clothes. I got rid of my abaya, headscarf and veil and put on a short skirt and slinky blouse.'

But that was not the most significant event of Lula's time in Paris.

At the Louvre her Algerian friend, who was also taking part in the session, whispered that the man contemplating the Mona Lisa was a famous painter, and that just a few days ago one of his paintings had sold at auction for a record figure, much more than any of the auction houses had seen in the past five years.

Lula decided to make a record of her Parisian adventure, taping herself on the old cassette player. It seemed to me that she was mocking 'Abd al-Raqeeb, who'd begun to record his own sermons in classical Arabic to develop his skills as a preacher. She didn't say this. Perhaps there were other reasons – I didn't ask.

I stayed to listen during the recording:

A Personal Cassette Recording

'I wanted to get to know him. I'm not sure why.'

[I can clearly remember Lula's expression as she spoke, as though she were right here in front of me now, as I write down what she recorded].

'I went up to him and said in English, "Do you like the Mona Lisa?" He said "I like anything nude." "But the Mona Lisa isn't nude," I said to him. "Actually she is nude. Can't you tell?" he said. "No," I replied. He was silent for a moment, his eyes fixed on the painting. Then he turned to me and took a good, long look before asking me "Do you like tomatoes?" I told him that I did like them, especially pureed with hot peppers. Then he said "I want to paint you, with tomatoes." At first, I was really embarrassed, but I quickly got over it. "OK," I said, "on the condition you don't paint my real face." He didn't agree to my condition, telling me that art refuses any conditions – if it is produced according to conditions, it is no longer worthy of being called art.

My first thought was "What if the painting ever makes its way to Yemen, and Father sees it?" I felt nervous, confused. But a famous artist painting me? It was an opportunity. In a moment of recklessness, I found myself agreeing; or was it anger, or even courage? Call it what you will. "OK, OK,"

I said to him, which made a little smile appear on his lips, a cocky smile I guess. Actually, it was more mocking, but I saw something else in there too, though I couldn't put my finger on what exactly. Perhaps it was pity. Maybe he'd realised why I'd originally insisted that he didn't make my face recognisable. Perhaps he felt sorry for me when I dropped my only condition as quickly as I'd set it.'

[Me]'Then what happened?'

'We agreed that I'd come to his home studio at eight that evening. Andrew − that was his name − wrote his address on the palm of my left hand, in dark red ink.'

She took her time, choosing her words with care − very different to how she had been with the painter that evening. I felt Lula was afraid of what my reaction would be if she told me everything. But I was eager to hear the details. She said only that she went to him and they agreed she would come to Paris to work with him as a model for three months, from 21 June to 21 September, each year for the next three years. At this point she insisted we stop the tape and save the rest of the story for another time.

Her relationship with her old boss had become purely platonic. After the Paris trip, she no longer seemed to need his financial support, although she told my father she'd been given a pay rise. As far as he was concerned, this meant he could continue to rely on her support.

Later, when I insisted she finish her story about the French artist and his painting, she brought out the cassette recorder again, turned over the cassette − even though there was still space on the first side − and picked up from where she'd left off:

'He was a strange artist. When I went to him he asked

me to remove my clothes, just like that. It was like I'd just got over one embarrassing situation to find myself in another. He said this was the first time he'd seen an Eastern woman naked, in real life, not in pictures. Then he took me to the bathroom and asked me to get in the tub. I got a fright when I saw him opening a large tin and then begin pouring its contents all over me. He said "Pureed tomatoes, but no hot peppers I'm afraid," and then he took off all his clothes.

I think he must have been in his fifties, perhaps a little older. He got in the bath, putting one foot either side of my hips and squatting down over me. I thought he was going to fuck me, but instead he began to rub me with the tomato puree like he was trying to get it to stick to me, or the red to stain my skin. He began by putting his hands on my nipples, stroking them slowly and gently, then he caressed my face and my neck. He moved his hands back down, over my shoulders, arms, chest, belly until he reached down between my thighs. With the same gentle touch, he moved on down to my knees, ankles, then the soles of my feet and toes. He returned to my nipples, and this time his rubbing wasn't as gentle, but it was slower. Then he began to squeeze them, massaging them rhythmic- ally . . . What am I telling you! I need a coffee. I'll admit I was scared he was going to strangle me when he gripped my throat with all his fingers as he massaged it. Then he squeezed my clitoris and rubbed my pussy and the way he did it drove me wild. I got more and more turned on as he went harder and faster. I felt like a box of matches, his hand lighting one after the other. I screamed with pleasure. I tried to push myself towards him, towards his thing, but he just kept on touching me. Then he asked me to stand up and he began to dry me off with three red towels. When he'd finished this ritual, he took me into a cramped room that was obviously his studio. He sat me on a low table scattered with paintbrushes and covered with white sheets, and then took a brush and began to paint. He seemed tense as he made his brush strokes on the canvas in front of him. That wasn't all . . .'

Lula was silent for a moment, and then she switched off the recorder. The noise of the button is captured on the tape. She asked me to make her a cup of strong coffee. I wasn't about to say no – I wanted her to carry on with her story.

It seemed like a long story. Over the next few minutes, while she drank her coffee, our eyes kept furtively meeting. Then she resumed her story.

'He suddenly pulled down the first canvas and threw another one up in its place. Then he adjusted my pose so that I was leaning back on my arms. I arched my back and kept my shoulders straight so that I wouldn't lose my balance. He bent my legs at the knee and opened them so that the bit in between was clearly visible. Actually, he opened my legs as far as they would go. I thought he was going to paint my vagina. I was so embarrassed and couldn't stop thinking "What if this painting becomes famous and reaches Yemen, and Father sees it? What would he do if he learned that his daughter's pussy was famous?"

It wasn't easy to make out what he was painting. The intersecting lines formed a sort of a spider's web overlaid with soap bubbles and spots of bright colour: like drops of blood, sperm and burnt oil. Father wouldn't understand this kind of abstraction, but I did. His eyes were fixed on the spot between my thighs the whole time he was painting.

I knew the opening that filled the canvas like an exploding volcano must be my pussy. Oh – do you know what he did? He kept using his fingers to spread my lips and explore my opening. He studied my clitoris, which appeared to me, in the painting he produced, like a volcano's peak.

But the painting still wasn't finished. I kept twisting, my eyes moving between his brush strokes and his naked body. Actually, I was watching the way his penis, stiff like his brush, bobbed up and down. I don't think I'll ever forget what happened next. He still hadn't asked me to change my pose. So I stayed in position, trembling, wanting to jump on him, to put him on his back, grab his cock and ride him, to give him a good pounding. But what did he do? From under the table he took out another large tin of tomato puree and sat down beside me. He began painting my body again. And I'd thought he'd finished! I sat there moaning with longing as he spread the puree over my neck, breasts and between my thighs. I was going crazy. Without even thinking about it I found myself dipping my hand into the tin and spreading puree over his erect cock. He seemed to be enjoying it and turned to face me. I got even more turned on. I held his cock tight and pushed myself towards it, until the tip was above my clitoris. I thought I was helping him to finish the painting. But I was wrong. He stood up suddenly and slapped me across the face.'

[Me] 'God punish you! God curse you!'

'What? But we agreed!'

I didn't want her to talk about these things anymore. I'd got so worked up that I couldn't hide the moisture dripping between my thighs as Lula talked. She kept telling me to go and wash it off in the bathroom, confident of the effect her words were having on me.

The story hadn't ended as I'd expected. There was still one question that I couldn't let go of, but despite myself, I kept quiet.

Lula stopped the cassette player and went to get another tape.

Even though there was plenty of space left on the tape, she was afraid she would fill it before she could finish her story.

A Personal Cassette Recording (2)

'He'd discovered I was a virgin. He was stunned by the lock on my pussy. Imagine, he couldn't even be bothered to give his key a good push to open it and come inside.'

[Me] 'A virgin?! What are you on about? How can you be a virgin? What is this?'

'Yep, a virgin, my Muslim sister. Did you think your sister had lost her way? That her morals were base and corrupt? God forbid, God forbid. Do you think I could really disobey God, and not fear His punishment, His hell fire? And me, a paragon of virtue, a model of chastity. God willing, God willing!'

[Me] 'Without going on too much, and without mocking our religion, tell me, what happened?'

'Don't you believe that it's possible for a girl to get her virginity back once she's lost it? Listen, before the boss would agree to me travelling to Paris on my own he made me visit this Russian doctor, Natasha. At first I was surprised he even knew of her and I wasn't sure what he wanted exactly. But he took me in his car and dropped me off in front of her clinic. He waited for me there until I returned, a newly restored virgin. I travelled on the condition that I'd return to him stitched up tight, as God created me.'

[Me] 'Don't you dare speak God's name. God curse you!'

'My God, you're cursing me again. Enough. Don't you want me to finish?'

I thought the story had finished, or at least that things were clear now. I didn't ask her to continue.

After a few moments of silence, also caught on the tape, she started talking again, without any prompting from me:

'The flight to Paris stopped off at Jeddah. I only woke up because the air hostess asked me to sit upright in my chair and prepare for take-off again. I noticed a new passenger had taken the seat next to me. I don't know what it was that made him ask me "Where in Yemen are you from?" I'd already taken off my abaya in the bathroom. Was it because the plane was coming from Sana'a?

He apologised for disturbing me and introduced himself. His name was Ahmad and he was a Saudi who was studying computer programming in the States. He was going to visit his sister, who lived in Paris with her Spanish husband. We talked about everything. He made me feel at ease with his ideas on women's rights, but he lost me when he insisted that a girl should keep her honour intact. He said he could never marry or love, or even talk to a girl who had lost her honour. I said to him, laughing, "And how do you know I'm a virgin?" He said "You've got an honest face, even if you're not wearing a veil."

After we talked for a while longer, he asked me outright if I would marry him. He didn't waste much time! I thought he was joking. I told him he could never pay my dowry, as it was very expensive. But he wasn't put off, and told me that he was from a rich family with roots in the Hadramaut region of Yemen. He said he would pay any price, no matter how high. He gave me his sister's address in Paris, but we didn't agree on a specific date.

When I left Andrew's house he was screaming at me "Sick! Pathetic! Stitched up!" I sensed that was the end of my modelling for him. I thought about the young Saudi guy: Why not marry him? I'm a virgin now, aren't I? I went to him, to tell him that I'd accept his offer, on the condition we get to know each other a little first. He agreed, and invited me out to dinner. Afterwards we went back to his sister's place, and he did everything he possibly could to make me agree to giving him what he'd described as my "honour." At first I made a show of refusing. But he kept promising he'd marry me and was willing to give me any assurance I wanted. Do you know what he did once I'd given into him, and he'd established his prowess by tearing the threads of my honour? He took a bunch of notes out of his wallet and handed them to me without a word. I didn't know what was going on. I kept asking him "What's the money for?" Eventually he yelled "This is the price of your honour!" He added that he didn't want to marry a girl who was happy to give away her honour to the first man who came along. He kept yelling, even though I hadn't tried to argue with him. I didn't bother to remind him that he'd promised me marriage and that I'd taken him at his word. He told me he was testing me, and then passed judgement: "A woman who gives away her honour before marriage is a woman who cannot be trusted in marriage."'

[Me] 'So in the end, what happened?'

'A week later I went back to the artist. I'd recovered from the damage caused when my stitches were torn. I wanted to tell him I was no longer a virgin. But he refused to talk about it and gave me some money, which he said was compensation for breaking the contract between us. I told him virginity wasn't one of the clauses in the contract. He said that my stitches had ruined his mood, that they had hurt his thing, and that he couldn't look at me without picturing my stitched-up pussy.'

[Me] 'You poor thing, you lost both a potential husband and the chance to work with a famous artist.'

'That's not all, I also lost my relationship with my boss when he found out I was no longer the virgin Natasha had created.'

[The sound of me screaming] 'God punish you! What is this apostasy? Don't compare that infidel whore to the Creator!'

Side A of the Om Kalthoum tape (replay)

Ask my heart when it repents
Perhaps it will hold beauty to blame.

When we heard the Islamic University had accepted my application, 'Abd al-Raqeeb started calling me 'Sheikha,' and the rest of the family soon followed suit. With this title it seemed that I'd become someone the whole family could trust – my comings and goings were now my own business. For the first time in my life I felt free, but even this had its limits. The sharia I'd studied and learnt by heart set the bounds of my freedom. It became a part of my life, if not my whole life.

At university the students didn't really refer to one another by fancy titles, although the lecturers treated us like serious religious scholars. Umm al-Muhibb was the only student we referred to as 'Sheikha.' Within the first few days of term she had established herself as a knowledgeable student. Not only did she know the entire Quran off by heart, she could recite it properly, and explain it. She had even memorised over two hundred sayings of the Prophet Muhammad. The lecturers were amazed by her knowledge.

Our male lecturers instructed us via a video link. We only heard their voices and saw their hands writing on the blackboard – never their faces. But it was from these scant clues that we learnt to recognise them – the shape of their fingers and the way they moved them, their hand-writing, even how their sleeves hung around their wrists. Their rings were particularly useful for telling them apart. If there were a voice or a pair of hands we didn't recog-nise, then our classmate, Faten, would come to the rescue. Straight away, she'd be able to tell us his name or whether he was new.

She would usually laugh and say something like 'Your favourite, Sheikha Faten, at your service' – even though she knew no one else ever described her as a 'sheikha.' The title 'sheikha' meant a lot to us, so we didn't use it lightly. Most of the students were quite serious, except Faten, who said she had been enrolled against her will. Perhaps Saeeda had also been forced to study at the university, but unlike Faten she just stayed silent the whole time. She wouldn't even say hello, and only spoke if a lecturer asked her a question.

Ask a sensible man for sensible answers
But who could keep his wits in the face of such beauty?

If I were to ask my heart
Tears would answer in its place.

One day our Jurisprudence lecturer told us there was a fault with the video link and that we'd only be able to hear his voice. The same thing happened afterwards with the Islamic Education lecturer, only he suddenly appeared on screen in a way none of us could have expected:

A University Cultural Mobile Phone Recording

We were expecting the sheikh to continue the lesson on the Muslim family that he'd begun the week before, but he told us, 'I'd like to put the course book to one side for a moment and instead talk to you from the heart.' We all took out our pens and notebooks, apart from those of us who had a mobile phone to record the lesson on. The sheikh reminded us the camera was faulty and that we'd only be able to hear his voice: 'I tried directing the camera at the blackboard but I couldn't get it to focus, so I've had to leave it.'

It was clear the sheikh had played with the camera as it was now pointing at him, although at an odd angle. At first we could see the lower half of his face and chest. The image was cropped from just below his eyes to his stomach, which pressed against the desk. But even so, this was the first time any of us had been able to see one of our male lecturers.

His black beard looked smooth and silky. His honey-coloured moustache covered part of his upper lip, and the red of his lower lip was revealed as he spoke.

'Today I am going to talk about one of the most important ingredients for a successful marriage: the encounter between man and wife in the marital bed – as decreed by Almighty God in his noble Book and exemplified by His Prophet Muhammad, peace be upon him. We work on the principle that there is no shame in Religion. All of you will become wives and mothers one day.'

The expression 'there is no shame in Religion' got the students' attention, since they recognised it as the preamble to a delicate issue.

We also all noticed that, for the first time ever, he was speaking to us directly using the formal grammatical forms reserved for a group of women without any men among them. On previous occasions he'd always spoken to us as if we were a mixed or male group – using the masculine grammatical forms, following very formal Arabic convention – and simple phrases like 'know that' or 'you must' or 'I am telling you.'

The angle of the camera began to slowly dip until his face was no longer visible.

I remember that day so clearly. Our eyes had immediately been drawn to the red flush of his lips, but as he spoke they grew more and more attractive.

'Dear ladies, I am going to talk to you candidly, heart to heart. I want my words to reach young hearts filled with faith and the guidance of God's Prophet, peace be upon him.'

The way 'heart' rolled off the sheikh's tongue suggested it was a word he particularly relished. He began with the words of the Prophet, who had affirmed the groom-to-be's right to see his fiancée before the wedding: *'If he is able to look at what will induce him to marry her, he should do so.*[1]*'*

He went on to clarify for us what was meant:

'What the Prophet is telling us is that the groom should look at the woman's private parts, her very private parts, for us to see if these parts arouse our desire and attract us to what God has sanctified. If this is the case then we trust

<hr>

1   Hadith transmitted by Abu Dawud, trans. Sh. M. Ashraf.

in God and complete the wedding contract, but if she is not so, then we must withdraw, for God has chosen what is best for us.'

It looked like the camera had dipped even further. There was now a blurry image of what looked like a wooden stick – most likely a leg of the desk the sheikh was sitting at. The trembling white sheet also in shot was obviously his tunic, which hung down over his knees.

'Our noble Prophet had the best of intentions for women. He said: *But those [wives] from whom you fear arrogance – [first] advise them; [then if they persist], forsake them in bed; and [finally], strike them. But if they obey you [once more], seek no means against them.*[2] The term 'ill conduct' here means disobedience to the husband and saying bad things, not adultery, as some imagine, for which the punishment is more severe than a light beating. As God's Prophet said: *If a husband calls his wife to bed and she refuses and causes him to sleep in anger, the angels will curse her till morning.*'[3]

His voice rose as he spoke these last words, but he quickly regained his usual, calm tone.

'These are the morals of Islam. By being obedient to her husband, a woman wins his love and affection, and above all, she wins God's approval.'

He paused and cleared his throat as though he were preparing to say something particularly important.

'Likewise, Islam has given woman her sexual rights. The Prophet permitted one woman to ask for a divorce, after

---

2   Quran, Surah an-Nisa verse 34, trans. Abdullah Yusuf Ali.
    Exact meanings and interpretations of this verse are highly contested, with debate centred on whether or not physical violence is being referred to.
3   Hadith transmitted by al-Bukhari, trans. Muhammad Muhsin Khan.

she told him that her husband had only "the fringe of a garment," by which she meant his penis was as flaccid as a rag and did not become erect. Thus, according to the rules of Islam, married life should be filled with sexual satisfaction, with both partners fulfilling the needs of the other, without holding back. Husband and wife should lie naked together and caress one another. Our example is God's Prophet, who said to someone who was ashamed at his spouse seeing his private parts: *I see theirs and they see mine.*[4] So there is nothing to prohibit husband and wife from looking at each other's private parts, from touching and caressing them to ignite each other's passions for an intimate, romantic encounter.'

The lens had slipped even further and was now pointing directly at the lecturer's belly and knees. His hand, which gripped his gown between his thighs, stiffly and excitedly, brought into sharp focus exactly what was going on.

'God's Prophet, peace be upon him, used to kiss his wives a lot, on any and all parts of their bodies. It is told that he used to kiss some of his women before rising to pray. The sayings of the Prophet confirm that he would suck the tongue of his wife, Aisha, and that he used to put his mouth on hers while she fed him meat.'

I don't think I was the only one who was embarrassed, caught between watching the hand of the sheikh – our lecturer – as it maintained its stiff grip on what had expanded between his thighs, and writing down what I heard in my notebook. He spoke in a leisurely manner, as though deriving deep pleasure from the words themselves. His pace allowed me to write down every word he said,

---

4 Hadith transmitted by al-Tabarani in *al-Mu'ajam al-Kabir*, vol. 9, p.38.

while a couple of girls filmed the lecture on their mobile phones.

'Besides kissing and caressing, there is also what we call vulgar talk. This consists of spoken obscenities, uttered by the woman during sexual intercourse, in order to tease her husband and bend him to her desire, so that his passions are ignited and he responds similarly. It is said that the best of Arab women are those who show their affection for their husbands openly, and it is also said that the best of them grunt and snort during sexual intercourse. Islam permits intercourse in any position. A difference of opinion arose between the early Muslims who migrated from Mecca and the Prophet's supporters in Medina. Like the Jews of Medina, the Ansar – the Prophet's supporters – believed that a woman should be taken while lying on her side. But those who migrated to Medina from Mecca and belonged to the Quraysh – the Prophet's tribe – enjoyed and took pleasure in several positions, lying down, from the front or from behind. When one of the Quraysh married a woman from the Ansar, he wanted to enjoy her bent over. As Umm Salama, mother of the believers and wife of the Prophet, may God be pleased with her, said, this is when the woman bends over on her knees. But the woman from the Ansar refused until she asked God's Prophet, and he revealed God Almighty's words: *Your wives are as a tilth unto you; so approach your tilth when or how ye will.*[5]

The sheikh paused, although his hands continued to play with what was between his thighs.

With the exception of Umm Muhibb, who remained hunched over her writing and didn't look up, most of the

---

5   Quran, Surah al-Baqarah verse 223, trans. Abdullah Yusuf Ali.

girls' eyes were now glued to the screen. They only looked at their notebooks to jot down something they thought important, like the name of a writer related to the subject. Faten refused even to write down the important stuff and simply sat, transfixed, staring at the screen.

The sheikh cleared his throat, as though he'd suddenly remembered what he wanted to say. Or perhaps it was just the rustling of the piece of paper he now took from his pocket and began to read from.

'After the book of Almighty God and the sayings and example of His Prophet, peace be upon him, there are many books on the subject of sex in Islam. Last week I read a book called "*Sex in the Light of Islam*" by Sheikh Abu Ahmad al-Maati. It was this book that gave me the idea to talk to you on the subject. Since I am speaking of sexual matters, I want to stress the author's call for the freedom to enjoy all sexual positions so long as they meet the needs of both parties, and are enjoyed by them. The author mentions two positions which he cites from other books on the subject. I shall discuss them here, since they are beneficial both for enjoyment and in addressing sexual issues that many men and women face. The first is when the man lies on his back, bends his legs and opens them a little. The wife then mounts him like a horse. This is one of the positions desired by the woman, because it gives her freedom of movement in ways she finds stimulating, and brings her to a climax quickly, with no great effort required from the husband. When he is close to ejaculation he can flip her over and climb on top of her. As for the second position, this is useful if the man is quick to climax but the woman slow. He needs to engage in foreplay for longer, and cuddle her more, sucking on her lips and breasts, stroking her chest and buttocks. He kisses her neck and then slowly rubs her clitoris with his penis without penetrating her. When she is fully aroused and grips him tightly, he slips it in little by little until it is all the way in and then moves it vigorously inside her until her waters gush forth . . .'

I noticed the camera lens had paused. The frozen shot was explicit enough to be in a cultural film. Sheikha Umm al-Muhibb was no longer in her place. She might have left the room a good while ago for all I'd noticed. Most of the other students were on their way out of the room, but Faten remained in her seat, astonished. 'What's wrong with you?' I asked her.

She looked at me and then got up. We were the last to leave the room.

'There'll be no cucumbers, aubergines or bananas left in the market today,' Faten chuckled.

I pretended I didn't know what she was getting at.

'How many hungry pussies are going to suck on that fruit and veg without being satisfied . . .' She added.

How did I not know what these girls got up to when I had Lula for a sister, I asked myself – but I didn't want to say this out loud.

When I enquired about *Sex in the Light of Islam* at three separate bookshops close to the university, the booksellers were baffled. They had sold out of it just that day. I had to go to a bookshop further out of town to find a copy.

Even after she watched the mobile phone recording, Lula couldn't bring herself to believe what had happened. I found it odd when she told me it was a fabrication to smear men of faith, even though there was no love lost between her and them. Perhaps this is why the students never told a soul, even their families. They knew no one would believe them. Even among the girls, it was a long time before anyone dared mention what happened that day. In fact, I got the impression that all the students – myself included – hadn't dared to even think about it. It was as though it had never really happened.

A Personal Cassette Recording (3)

When 'Abd al-Raqeeb used to practice preaching, up in his room on the roof, the subject that occupied him more than any other was loose women. On the rare occasions he digressed from this subject, it was usually to talk about a wife's obedience to her husband. His voice could be heard loud and clear downstairs. No doubt he imagined himself ascending the pulpit of a large mosque and addressing his sermon to an enraptured audience. I can't really explain what I'm feeling as I listen back to his recording.

'Those loose women. Those women who do not stay at home as God has commanded them. Those women who flaunt their body's charms as though a second age of ignorance had come. Yes, a second age of ignorance. They go out shopping with their faces uncovered, stinking of perfume, tempting men with their painted faces, swarming upon them like the devil. Those women who mock God's law and the example of His Prophet. Where will they hide from God's punishment? Where? Where will they hide? Where? They are heading for eternal damnation – in hell!'

He didn't neglect to mention those faithful and compliant women who guard their chastity and obey their lord husbands. As he tested out the sound of his voice he'd often say the same things over and over again, so that I ended up unintentionally knowing most of it by heart.

'Consider Almighty and Exalted God's word in the Noble Quran. Is there anything more sacred than the word of God? [He says this in a loud and impassioned voice.]

'He – Mighty and Majestic – says' [lowering his voice] 'in the Surah of Women: *Men are the protectors and maintainers of women, because Allah has given the one more (strength) than the other, and because they support them from their means.*[6] And in the Surah of the Cow, He – May He be exalted – says: *men have a degree (of advantage) over them.*[7]'

[Raising his voice again] 'This is the word of God. God's law says that the male has twice the share of the female. Clearly, clearly God has defined woman's place . . . Islam preserves woman's dignity and honour when it orders her to stay at home, obedient to her husband . . . Indeed, the Prophet, who did not speak from his own inclination but from revelation revealed, said . . . Listen to what he said . . . He said: *Were I to command someone to prostrate himself before another, I would command the wife to prostrate herself before her husband.*[8] You see? The Prophet ordered woman to be obedient to her husband to the extent that he almost asked her to bow down before him. Those are the words of the Prophet, God's beloved and the last of the Prophets, not the words of the government and its infidel, secular laws. This is God's law, not the law of those drunken fornicators who spend the night in the arms of harlots and in the

6 Quran, Surah an-Nisa, verse 34, trans. Abdullah Yusuf Ali.
7 Quran, Surah al-Baqara, verse 228, trans. Abdullah Yusuf Ali.
8 Hadith transmitted by Abu Dawood, trans. Madelain Farah in *Al-Ghazali: Marriage Sexuality in Islam*

morning call for women's liberation, for her to be able to leave the house whenever she pleases. They hide from people's sight by night but they do not realise that the eye of God sees them, awake and never sleeping.'

Women became 'Abd al-Raqeeb's preoccupation. One of the earliest things I memorised was 'Most women who enter the fires of hell do so because of their disobedience to their husband and their ingratitude towards his goodness.' It was only later that we learnt that this wasn't something 'Abd al-Raqeeb had come up with himself, when once he began with: 'God's Prophet said—'[9] Still, all these sermons never managed to erase the image of the old Raqeeb from my memory, when, after getting drunk on one of his quarts, he would encourage me to free myself from everything.

Time to listen to the song again.

Ask a sensible man for sensible answers
But who could keep his wits in the face of such beauty?

If I were to ask my heart
Tears would answer in its place.

In my chest there is only flesh and blood
Feeble now that youth has gone.

My heart weeps and I say: It's over
In my chest it trembles and I say: Repent!

---

9   This is in fact not a hadith but a quote from *Fiqh al-Sunna,* a famous book on Islamic law by the Egyptian religious scholar Sheikh El-Sayyid Sabiq el-Tihami (1915-2000).

Lula was still the family's main provider. I don't know how we managed to get by before she started working. As well as paying for pretty much all the food, she would also pay for the khat my father used to chew. His salary was spent by the middle of the month. He showed his gratitude by never asking Lula about her comings and goings. When 'Abd al-Raqeeb began to ask why she was getting home so late in the evenings and travelling abroard without a male guardian, my father said to him, 'As long as I'm alive it's no one else's business. I'm her father.'

These words, which he often repeated, would come to take on a much deeper significance. When the surgeons who operated on his heart confirmed that Lula's actions had saved him from certain death, he was not only grateful, he felt he owed her his life. She paid for him to be treated in Jordan, all at her own expense. In Sana'a three different doctors had told him that if he didn't travel and have the operation within ten days the situation would become critical.

On the day he returned home he addressed us all solemnly: 'Everyone be here after the sunset prayer. I have something I want to say to you.'

That afternoon we all stayed close to his bed, waiting anxiously to hear what he had to say. At the appointed time, he called each of us by name to make sure we were all present. Closing his eyes he said feebly: 'My advice to you all . . . My only advice to you . . . Listen 'Abd al-Raqeeb . . . No one has the right to interfere in Lula's business as long as I'm alive . . . And even when I'm gone no one has the right to interfere in her business . . . Her business is her own . . . None of you have the right to judge her . . . Have you all got that?'

Over the following months my father would often say that he was only alive thanks to the grace of God who gave him his daughter, Lula, so that she could save his life. I noticed a little smile on her lips every time he said this. Later, she would reply: 'Everything is thanks to Him. Yes, His grace. By His grace.' I used to think, and probably the others too, that she meant God, but after a while I discovered she meant something else. I noticed that every time she said this she would press the palm of her right hand between her thighs, over the spot to which the credit was due.

In my chest there is only flesh and blood
Feeble now that youth has gone.

My heart weeps and I say: It's over
In my chest it trembles and I say: Repent!

We were expecting a definitive opinion from the university chancellor on the fatwas that Sheikh al-Marwi had issued in his lecture, but this is not what happened. The chancellor made do with a terse statement published in the university newspaper: 'The time was inappropriate to issue such fatwas when students are approaching their exams at the end of the first semester, a time when they need to focus on their classes and revision, without such disruptions.'

The Student Activities Department had devised a weekly open day. Every Thursday the Department would invite a sheikh or some other religious authority from outside the university to give a lecture on whatever topic he thought appropriate.

'Does the university chancellor agree with Sheikh Marwi's fatwas when he says the timing was inappropriate?

Does that mean they would have been acceptable if he'd issued them at any other time? And if he said the students need to focus on their classes and revision without disruption, does that mean these fatwas are merely a disruption, a fuss that will soon die down?' The female students and lecturers continued to ask each other such questions without arriving at any answers. I had no idea if the same questions were being asked in the men's section.

The chancellor's fears that the sheikh's pronouncements might prove disruptive for some students were well founded. With all the fuss, I couldn't stop replaying a recording of his lecture.

A Mobile Phone Recording (Fatwas)

'Some fathers are stuck in the age of ignorance and need to acquaint themselves with Islam. They name their daughters Jameela, Fatina, Ghaniya . . . Provocative names that expose what God has veiled in woman. There is no God but God. This is the state of Islam at the end of time. We call her Jameela, Fatina – such decadence! It's as though we were at a slave market, advertising this and that pretty slave girl.'

He continued to expound: 'Such names go against the way of Islam and the way of God's law. Only an infidel would give his daughter such a name. In a previous lecture I said that these names are the result of the Western cultural attack on our Islamic values – through television, soap operas, films . . . and now the internet. The newest weapon in the war on Islam is the Internet. Through the songs and dirty pictures they share on their mobile phones. Bluetooth. Yes,

Bluetooth. The sincere Muslim, the true Muslim must protect his faith, his family and the greater Muslim family. But how?'

The sheikh gave his fatwa – his definitive answer: 'This can only be done by destroying the phones equipped with Bluetooth, smashing the satellite dishes and internet devices. Computers are the idols of this age. We must smash them in the same way the first Muslims smashed the idols of the polytheists in the holy city of Mecca.'

The sheikh hadn't failed to include in his pronouncements the very means by which the recording of his lecture was transmitted to others, Bluetooth.

Apparently, one of the students from the male section of the university had recorded the lecture on his mobile phone. Every time I went back to the recording, sent to Lula's phone that same day, I found myself asking a number of questions. Not only had his opinions on women's education left me with a whole load of questions, I became totally confused when I tried to reconcile them with my own convictions.

'What do we gain from woman when we call on her to study at primary school, secondary school, or university? Isn't it enough for her to study until she turns nine? This is the age at which it is permitted for a girl to marry, as in the example set by God's Messenger, Muhammad, peace be upon him, who married Aisha when she was nine years old. To educate her after this age would have meant her leaving the house and coming into contact with other men. This is against God's teachings, which instruct women to remain at home. The schoolgirl becomes a woman when she turns nine. Let Aisha, Mother of the faithful, may God be pleased with her, be an example for all God-fearing women. Her marriage to the Prophet at this age was an obligatory practice that we must follow. As the popular expression goes' [he lowers his voice and chuckles] "Marry a girl of eight, and I'll give you a guarantee." So it is not acceptable, not acceptable' [now raising his voice] 'for us to remain silent while we watch girls mix with boys at the colleges, or female teachers teach boys at primary school with the excuse that they're just children. What if a boy grows up and remembers his female teacher?' [He pauses for a moment]. 'Sadly, and I say sadly' [lowering his voice] 'yes, I say sadly' [raising his voice again] 'even those universities and colleges that call themselves Islamic have opened up departments for female students. In the name of Islam they go against Islam. Is it right that we should hear the voice of a woman, even if she is reading from the Quran? We know that a woman's voice is private, so then how has it come to this? We've opened colleges to teach Quran so that women's voices can be heard by men. The hurma's voice is haram! It is the voice of temptation, the voice of the devil, tempting us away from God's word. Instead of listening to God's word and contemplating its meaning, we listen to their sweet voices and are bewitched by their feminine beauty. There is no God but God. May God put an end to such an abomination!'

Some of the male students were clearly moved by the sheikh's impassioned delivery – they could be heard on the recording repeating 'Amen, Amen' after his prayer.

A Cultural Videocassette (Personal)

Lula insisted I come with her to the home of one of her workmates. When I realised they were going to watch a

cultural film, or a sex film, I got up to leave. They clung
to me, begging me to stay. I put my hands over my eyes
and tried to move away from the television.

Everyone had started calling me 'Sheikha,' so how could
I be party to such things, now that I'd taken this new path
in life so at odds with the way Lula lived hers?

Lula tried to prise my hands away from my eyes. I was
sure we were going to end up fighting, but she switched
tactics. Soothingly, she said: 'Listen. Please, just listen. I only
want you to know what's in the film. You don't need to
watch the whole thing. This is a different film. It's different.
True, it's a film, but the people in it aren't strangers. You
know the people in it. It's local sex.'

'And what difference does it make to me if it's local
or foreign?' I said as I tried to pull away towards the door.

'Wait. What's wrong with you? Just take a quick look
then decide for yourself. The film's not just local, the
people in it look like people you know. Please, just take
a look.'

'There, I'm looking – see?' I snapped, as I moved my
hands away and opened my eyes. I'd only intended to
humour Lula so she'd let me go, but nothing could have
prepared me for the scene my eyes collided with. The face
of the woman who moved up and down on the man was
familiar. In fact, I knew it well, very well. The camera moved
down from her face to her breasts and belly, focusing on
her naked torso. For a moment, the sheer shock of it caused
me to forget her name, or the place it occupied in my
memory shrank in embarrassment. It was Nura. The woman
didn't just resemble her, it really was her. I opened my
eyes wider, trying to discover who was beneath her. It
looked like 'Abd al-Raqeeb, but I couldn't be certain. The

cameraman was focussing more on Nura's body than on the man. Lula explained that it was 'Abd al-Raqeeb and Nura, and that they were on the roof of our house, outside their bedroom. She pointed out the evidence, such as the bed and the background – the door to their bedroom and the electric light, until I too became convinced it was them.

'What are we going to do?'

I didn't have an answer to Lula's question. All we could do was agree not to tell anyone and talk to Nura.

When Nura was shown the videotape, a look of bewilderment and then terror came over her face. She was speechless. It was as though she were watching a life she had lived without knowing it. Her expression now was very different to how it was in the film, as she moaned and panted, ecstatically: 'Ah, ah, ah . . .'

We spent the following two days in a state of utter confusion, as if under a spell. It was only broken by 'Abd al-Raqeeb hammering on the front door, so unlike the gentle knocking we were used to hearing whenever he returned from the mosque, where he prayed each of the five daily prayers.

That whoever was at the door had hammered instead of knocking meant it could only be Raqeeb.

Lula got up to let him in. As she left the bedroom Nura and I locked the door behind her.

'Where is she? Where is that daughter of a whore? Where is she? I knew that girl was nothing but a whore.'

Nura and I huddled behind the bedroom door trying to catch what he was saying. We pressed our hands against the lock as though to reinforce it.

'Calm down, son. What's wrong with you? What is it?' said Mother.

'Pray to the Prophet! What's wrong with you? You're a God-fearing man. Who filmed you like that?'

'She doesn't know. I swear to you on my life, she had nothing to do with it!' said Lula, realising what was at the heart of his anger.

'What do you mean, who filmed us? The whore was filmed with one of her lovers. She's an adulteress. Everyone's seen it.'

"Abd al-Raqeeb, what are you saying? Calm down. I'm sure it's you that's with her. What's important right now is for us to find out who filmed you.'

We could hear Father's voice somewhere in the background as he tried to find out what on earth was going on. Mother, on the other hand, was being rudely brought up to speed on everything we'd managed to keep from her.

Earlier, the three of us had concluded that one of the neighbours must have filmed them. It had probably happened on one of those sweltering summer nights when, unable to bear the heat inside their room, 'Abd al-Raqeeb and Lula slept on the roof. Our suspicions fell on the two houses that overlooked ours. Al-Jadha's sons were the most likely culprits since they were notorious for harassing the neighbourhood girls. But 'Abd al-Raqeeb refused to accept our theory, and only Father could convince him not to go through with his idea of killing Nura: 'Divorce her, don't kill her.'

'Abd al-Raqeeb let her go back to her parent's house, on the understanding that he would send her the divorce papers later.

'As soon as he recognised Nura he was blinded,' said Lula. 'If only he'd watched more than the first few seconds of the film, he would have seen that the man with Nura was him.' She could find no other reason to explain 'Abd al-Raqeeb's behaviour. She continued to elaborate on her theory, telling us she thought the video had been cunningly shot and edited, since it wasn't easy to make out 'Abd al-Raqeeb, while there was no mistaking Nura.

Nura's lusty panting became the talk of the neighbourhood, perhaps even the whole city, whether people had seen the video or not. Most of the people we knew directed their questions at our relatives, trying to find out whether the naked woman in the film really was Nura. A few satisfied themselves by simply staring us in the face. I found them more disconcerting than those who asked their questions out loud. Their silent stares seemed to hold more judgements and foregone conclusions than questions.

After Father sent Nura home to her family, we spent the rest of the night trying to calm down 'Abd al-Raqeeb.

The following morning we were awoken by a loud knocking on the front door. We looked out of the window to see armed men leading Nura out of her house and into a military vehicle. They sat 'Abd al-Raqeeb next to her, having led him out in his pyjamas. We had no idea where they were taking them.

I'm going to listen to Om Kalthoum now.

Even if hearts were made of iron
Still none could bear what mine has suffered.

No one can tell you about life's hardships
Like someone who has lost their loved ones.

Those who are dazzled by the riches of this world
Should know that I wore its finery until it fell to rags.

Three months and two days later 'Abd al-Raqeeb was
released from prison. Nura spent just ten days in the
women's prison and then she moved back to her parent's
house, where she lived alone. Her parents had gone to live
in Michigan with their son who'd married there and was
now an American citizen, and had left her the keys to the
family home. She refused to set foot inside our house again
unless it was to collect the divorce papers from 'Abd
al-Raqeeb. For a few weeks Lula slept over at Nura's to
keep her company.

None of us knew exactly why 'Abd al-Raqeeb refused
to divorce Nura after his release. The night he discovered
the tape, he hadn't wanted to divorce her, or get her out
of his life – he'd wanted to separate her from her life.

'You only admitted it was you in the film with Nura
and not some other man when it was too late, and even
then you didn't seem all that convinced. How can you
expect her to stay married to you?' Lula said, trying everything she could to convince him to give Nura a divorce.
She told 'Abd al-Raqeeb what she and Nura had done to
save him from the torture of the investigators at the Criminal
Investigation and Political Security Departments, so that
he'd be released quickly and without having to face trial.
She believed he ought to follow her advice in exchange
for everything she'd done for him: 'They wanted to hand
your case to the Deputy General, and charge you with the
production and distribution of pornographic material.
You just don't know. I couldn't have got you out of
prison without Nura's help, and she only did it on the condition you'd divorce her the moment you were released.
You'd be better off if you just divorced her now.'

'Abd al-Raqeeb became depressed and taciturn. He

refused to go and ask about the job he'd been absent from the whole time he was in prison. He would emerge from his room on the roof when we called him to dinner, and then quickly disappear back inside again. Lula kept bursting into his room and demanding he give Nura what she wanted. One evening we had a surprise visit from Nura, accompanied by Lula. When we saw her go straight up to the roof, we thought the river had returned to its course and that husband and wife had made up. Mother and Father were overjoyed, and perhaps even I was too. But Lula didn't let us get too carried away. In a whisper, she invited us to come and stand behind the door to 'Abd al-Raqeeb's room, so that we could hear what was being said.

'Look, you've got two choices, either you divorce me, or I divorce you.' Nura spoke in a clear voice and we were struck by how calmly she delivered her ultimatum. How could she divorce him? It was clear Lula didn't share our astonishment, and her knowing smile also suggested she was in on some kind of trick.

'I'm giving you twenty-four hours. I'll be here the same time tomorrow and you'd better be ready with an answer.'

Father tried to placate Nura and get her to explain exactly what she'd meant, but she refused outright his invitation to stay and have dinner with us. When Mother suggested Lula go back home with her so she wouldn't be alone, Nura just nodded and left without waiting for Lula.

From its gardens I gathered roses and thorns
And from its cup I tasted honey and resin.

We spent the following day on tenterhooks as we waited for Nura. Mother and Father both tried to make light of her threat. Father kept saying 'A woman has never divorced her husband,' as though to reconfirm his convictions, which Nura had clearly shaken. When she arrived at the house, exactly on time, Father was anxious to know what had been decided. He called up to 'Abd al-Raqeeb after Nura said she wanted to end the matter in front of the family, but 'Abd al-Raqeeb wouldn't answer, and just stayed in his room.

'Well, what have you decided? Come on. Come and divorce me,' Nura said after knocking on his door while we stood next to her on the roof. 'Come and divorce me,' she said again, louder this time. 'Abd al-Raqeeb seemed completely indifferent, his eyes fixed on the pages of a book. 'Come and divorce me!' She said so loudly I thought the neighbours must have heard. Nura didn't wait long. 'Abd al-Raqeeb's apparent nonchalance, the way he acted as though he hadn't even noticed her – or in fact any of us – had made her furious. She shook her head twice, like someone about to make a pledge or preparing to swear an oath on something.

> *From its gardens I gathered roses and thorns*
> *And from its cup I tasted honey and resin.*
>
> *But no wiser judgment than God's have I witnessed*
> *And no door other than His have I sought.*

She reached into her handbag and pulled something out. 'These are your divorce papers,' she said loudly. Then she said 'I divorce you, I divorce you, I divorce you,' and threw the papers at him as she left the room.

★

After asking Lula a million questions Father was finally convinced there was no going back; his son was now divorced. She assured him that the court's ruling − exceptional since it had been initiated by the wife − was legally sound, removing any last doubts. 'She divorced him in exchange for waiving his final payment towards the dowery. He has the right to demand additional financial compensation and appeal on this basis, but there's no going back on the divorce. That Nura, she's discovered she has abilities like no other woman.'

'Even you?' Father asked her. She giggled, as though he hadn't asked her a question but tickled her. When I was alone with Lula, I asked her about these abilities our brother's ex-wife was blessed with. 'What other abilities could there be?' she said, pressing her hand between her thighs. I couldn't believe Nura would have anything to do with this sort of thing, and so I kept questioning Lula until she told me the details of what happened to Nura while she was in prison, and how her abilities had influenced the outcome. She seemed irritated as she spoke, perhaps because the part these abilities had played had not been recognised: 'If it wasn't for Nura, if it wasn't for these abilities, then your dear brother would still be languishing in prison, with or without a trial.'

Side B of the song

I'm playing the song again, and this time I'm really focusing on the lyrics as I try to work out exactly why our neighbour gave me the tape.

From its gardens I gathered roses and thorns
And from its cup I tasted honey and resin.

But no wiser judgment than God's have I witnessed
And no door other than His have I sought.

'Resin' is a strange word. What could she mean? She gathered flowers and thorns . . . tasted honey, which is sweet. So I guess, by resin, she means bitter?

Nothing in life is worthier than kindness
Its blessings outlive the giver.

The Prophet of kindness showed the way
He led by example, guiding the people.

What is she saying? The kindness shown by the Prophet is the best and most enduring; it's the path he guided people along. These are beautiful words, words in praise of the Prophet. They don't conflict with Islam. Why haven't I listened to this tape before? I thought it was a love song. All Om Kalthoum's songs are about love, aren't they? At least that's what they say, and what I thought . . . Seems I was wrong.

> *Nothing in life is worthier than kindness*
> *Its blessings outlive the giver.*
>
> *The Prophet of kindness showed the way*
> *He led by example, guiding the people.*
>
> *His message was a path to the light*
> *His horses rode forth in the cause of right.*
>
> *He taught us how to gain glory*
> *So that we took command of the land by force.*
>
> *Demands are not met by wishing*
> *The world can only be won through struggle.*

So she's singing about the Prophet, the one who showed us the True Path, in the cause of which he sent his horses off to jihad. It was Muhammad, peace be upon him, who taught us to gain glory, even if this meant the Muslims had to take the land by force. He taught us to take power by force. We seize it. We take it by force. We fight the idolatrous infidels. It's no good just wishing. Our demands won't be met simply by wishing, but through determination, force, and conquest. Oh, how beautiful this poetry is! The Prophet teaches us to be determined and steadfast.

> *His message was a path to the light*
> *His horses rode forth in the cause of right.*
>
> *He taught us how to gain glory*
> *So that we took command of the land by force.*
>
> *Demands are not met by wishing*
> *The world can only be won through struggle.*

Could the song have another meaning? Didn't the Arabic teacher at the academy tell us the meaning of a line of poetry is in the belly of the poet?

> *Nothing is beyond the reach of a people*
> *When their feet are firmly in the stirrups.*

Such beautiful words . . . How slow am I? Why haven't I appreciated the beauty of these words before? There's nothing a people can't do if they set their sights on it and really go for it. Nothing is impossible.

> *Nothing is beyond the reach of a people*
> *When their feet are firmly in the stirrups.*
>
> *Abu al-Zahra, I've overstepped my rank*
> *In praising you, yet I seek the honour.*

She sings these last two lines so beautifully – how fluidly she moves from one to the next! Her voice is magnificent . . . the way she sings 'Abu al-Zahra' – 'father of al-Zahra' – a name for Muhammad, peace be upon him. Al-Zahra . . . as in Fatima Al-Zahra, the Prophet's daughter? I'm going to play this bit over and over again.

He taught us how to gain glory
So that we took command of the land by force.

Before 'Abd al-Raqeeb found religion, he'd tell me: 'If you want to play the game and have a presence then you've got to play at the designated time, exactly like in football. Don't play in stoppage or extra time. And if you can't play at the right time, then find another game to play. Never allow yourself to be sidelined.'

Whenever he drank one of his 'quarts,' as he called them, he would transform into another being, like a bird with boundless freedom.

He used to get the quart of moonshine from a friend, as he liked to tell me. Once back in his room on the roof, he'd use his teeth to tear open a corner of the sealed plastic bag his friend had delivered the quart in, and decant it into a plastic bottle. He'd slowly sip it, after diluting it a little with water. With the exception of Lula and I, no one else knew about Raqeeb's weekly habit. When he drank he was always careful to keep his distance from Mother and Father. Sometimes, he would break with tradition and drink almost every day, but this usually only happened when his social life was particularly busy or he'd managed to pester Lula into loaning him the money for a quart – a cursed loan, as I used to tell them.

I don't know. When he told me one of his 'brothers' had asked to marry me, had this been his idea of playing at the 'right time'? Or was it that the only opportunity he'd found for me to play was in stoppage time – lost time?

> *Demands are not met by wishing*
> *The world can only be won through struggle.*

I never really had the opportunity to play in the first place, so I never really had a choice. I agreed to marry 'Abd al-Raqeeb's friend, having no idea what role I would play in the game. 'It's better to play in stoppage time than not at all,' I tried to convince myself.

'Abd al-Raqeeb insisted that my suitor come and take a look at me before the marriage contract was completed. He said this was an obligation in the eyes of religion. I agreed, and got ready. But when my groom turned up – with his skinny young body and long wispy beard – he didn't look at me, didn't so much as steal a glance in my direction. He seemed painfully shy, and spent the few minutes or so he was in our house looking down at the floor, his eyes almost closed, murmuring: 'Praise be to God. Praise be to God. May God choose what is best for us and what pleases Him'.

Demands are not met by wishing

My wedding night wasn't easy. I reread the books about marriage and married life according to the Quran and the Prophet's example, but they didn't really prepare me. They helped me get over the usual embarrassment a bride faces on her wedding night, but they didn't mention anything about the kind of duties that need to be performed before sexual intercourse can lawfully take place. While the groom was performing his ablutions, preparing to pray, I changed out of my wedding dress and into my nightie, put on some perfume and touched up my make-up, as Mother and her friends had advised me. As soon as I lay down on the bed, my new husband Abu Abdullah spread the prayer rug out on the bedroom floor and prayed. 'May God accept your prayers,' I said to him. 'May God accept all our prayers,' he replied, and added, 'May God Guide you. Come and pray for God to bless our marriage and grant us virtuous off-spring, God willing.'

I did as he asked – well, it was more like an order. Then I checked my make-up again and gave myself another spray of perfume. He took off his short white tunic, but kept on his vest and the baggy white trousers that reached down to his ankles. He looked embarrassed, and tried to avert his eyes from my body. The flimsy nightie stopped at the top of my thighs and only partially covered my breasts. I tried to draw his attention to the details of my naked body – my legs and thighs, my long hair that flowed in two plaits down to my waist. I smiled expectantly, my neck anointed with fine Arabic scents prescribed by my sharia-abiding sisters.

But instead of leaning in to inhale my scent he just stood there, repeating, 'Praise be to God. Praise be to God. God has willed it. Praise be to God.' I didn't know of anything in sharia that should have prevented him from opening his eyes to look at me. He sat down on the bed beside me while I lay on my back, waiting for him to take the initiative.

Nothing is beyond the reach of a people

When he bent down on his knees and pulled open my legs, I remembered what I'd read about foreplay. But when he just pulled down my knickers and yanked down his trousers I realised that foreplay was just an idea in books, and nothing more. Even the cultural films I'd seen didn't seem to feature much foreplay.

His member looked lifeless, comatose. Even so, he kept hold of it with his left hand and pushed it towards the place between my thighs. Before embarking on this step, he'd recited various prayers and verses from Quran, beginning with: 'I take refuge in God from the Devil, in the name of God the most Gracious, the most Merciful.' I was embarrassed because I didn't know how to respond. He seemed to be observing some religious practice that was either compulsory or strongly favoured by sharia.

'Oh God, shield us from Satan and keep him away from us and from the things You bestow upon us. O God, I ask You for the goodness within her and the goodness that she is inclined towards, and I seek refuge with you from the evil to which she is inclined.'

I'd once heard there was a prayer called 'the marriage prayer.' Was this what he was reciting?

Pushing these thoughts aside, I began to move my lips, trying to give the impression I was quietly reciting prayers and verses from the Quran. I was worried my ignorance of things would upset him, especially if they were ordained by sharia. But none of this would matter once we were done with the preamble and came together in the act. I imagined that he would most likely expect me to lie still, a passive object, while he engaged in the act. 'I take refuge in God from Satan, in the name of God the most Gracious, the most Merciful,' he repeated at least ten times, while he held his member and pushed it towards my vagina. It wasn't long before I realised he was incapable of crossing the threshold, even though I'd opened the door wide, without him even bothering to knock.

> *Demands are not met by wishing*
> *The world can only be won through struggle.*

Mother devised a special diet for Abu Abdullah that would make him strong and help him overcome his difficulties. She was so concerned about his impotence that she told Lula about it, even though I'd begged her not to. Whenever we met it was always the first topic of conversation. Mother would whisper, 'Has he managed it yet or is it still no better?' 'No better,' I'd reply with a giggle, loud enough for Lula to hear, so she wouldn't ask me the same question in her own special way: 'Hey Pipsqueak, what's up? Any zeet-meet in your life yet?'

Lula had zeet-meet on the brain. She handed me a pill and told me to dissolve it in a glass of orange juice and give it to Abu Abdullah without telling him. At first I was hesitant, but for how long was I supposed to go without zeet-meet? I wanted to feel alive, to taste life.

Abu Abdullah ate a lot of Dawani honey, which he said was brought specially for him from the Hadramaut region in the south of Yemen. I would also see him eating some sort of paste from a jar labelled 'Groom Mix.' One day a package arrived for him with something small and red inside. 'This is a Korean herb. They say it's very effective, God willing.' He took a piece of it and after half an hour took another. 'I'm scared there'll be side effects if I take too much,' he said, and continued to reach into the packet until he'd eaten the whole lot. He was irritable and depressed. He'd staked a lot on the Korean herb and when it failed he seemed to reach the limits of despair.

Perhaps for once I genuinely felt sorry for him. 'It's OK, my love. It's doesn't matter. Physical intimacy isn't everything. Let's wash, and say an extra prayer, then get some sleep,' I said.

That was the first time I had called Abu Abdullah 'my love.' The second time was when he had a panic attack and fainted after taking the blue pill I'd dissolved in his orange juice. I was terrified – I thought he was dead. I cursed Lula and her stupid advice, and I broke down, wailing and sobbing words of affection I'd never used before. When 'Abd al-Raqeeb and Father rushed him to the hospital I told myself that if he lived I'd never get fed up with him again. I felt I'd lost the man of my dreams, forever. Strangely, this feeling didn't leave me, even after he returned from hospital alive and well, but actually got stronger with each passing day. I started to feel like a widow, but not a widow who had lost her husband – one who hadn't even been truly married in the first place.

> *Nothing is beyond the reach of a people*
> *When their feet are firmly in the stirrups.*

'Why?' I asked Abu Abdullah. He'd just told me: 'From now on there'll be no more university. They make so many mistakes when they teach sharia, especially how they teach it to the harem.' 'Harem' was his way of referring to women. We'd never discussed my studies, and I hadn't felt the need to ask

him if I could go and register for my second year. He just
came out with it, and wouldn't answer me when I asked
him why. He'd just say 'A hurma must obey her husband.'

His words made me think of Sheikh al-Marwi's fatwa.
Perhaps Abu Abdullah sensed from my expression that I
wasn't entirely convinced by his decision. He quickly added:
'There are differing opinions among the jurists and the
religious scholars on the subject. Many of them believe
educating a girl over the age of nine is inappropriate, because
that's when she becomes a hurma. Her place is in the home,
and she shouldn't leave it other than for the grave.'

I knew opinions differed. I can still remember what
the jurisprudence professor told us in our first lecture at
university: 'A man might be filled with pride when the
doctors tell him his hurma is pregnant with a boy, but what
he does not realise is that God has the power to turn a
male foetus into a female at any moment.' A female student,
clearly miffed at the professor's words, muttered: 'The
doctors themselves could change a male into a female or
vice versa.' This was Faten, who I'd get to know later. The
professor didn't hear her. He continued his lecture; or rather,
he continued to issue his fatwas. We can listen to what he
said on my mobile phone – someone sent me the recording
by Bluetooth.

A Mobile Phone Recording (Fatwas 2)

'It is not permitted for a pregnant *hurma* to be examined,
whether by a male or a female doctor. To examine her is
to expose a hurma, and this is forbidden. Only infidels

allow such things. If she is pregnant with a male foetus – the medical equipment having established this – and later, by God's will, the foetus transforms into a female, then here is the crime. And this crime is twofold. It is doubled because two hurmas have been violated – the pregnant hurma and the hurma in her womb. We have inherited our venerable Islamic customs from our fathers and our grandfathers and their fathers before them. We know that a woman remains a hurma even in death. She is mentioned by name only when this is unavoidable, because to mention her is an act of immodesty, and modesty is a part of faith. A man without faith is a man without modesty. Any man who talks about his hurma has lost his modesty and therefore his faith.'

Even without the recording, I can clearly remember writing in my notebook the last thing the professor said: 'The female is a hurma before birth, in life, and in death.'

Abu al-Zahra, I've overstepped my rank
In praising you, yet I seek the honour.

No man can claim eloquence
Unless he finds its source in you.

I have praised kings and risen high in their esteem
But when I praise you I rise above the clouds.

I pray to God for the children of my religion
May He hear and grant my prayers

In times of trouble and adversity
You are the Muslims' sole refuge.

I no longer left the house. Instead, I spent my days cooking and cleaning, usually while listening to Quran or cassette sermons. I stopped only when it was time to pray. In addition to the five obligatory prayers, I'd also pray the optional *duha*, *witr*, and *tajahud* prayers, as well as the decision-making prayer, said at times of difficulty or confusion. I also performed the prayer of need, which I heard some religious scholars have prohibited, considering it an innovation, and not an original part of the faith. But I felt a real need to say this prayer. An extra prayer won't hurt God. And anyway, I said to myself, isn't it called the 'prayer of need'?

I prayed that God would meet my unspoken need. That he would make my husband strong and we could enjoy a happy, contented life together. Of course, I never said this prayer in front of Abu Abdullah.

Sometimes I'd switch on the mobile phone Abu Abdullah had given me. It had lots of recorded lectures saved on it, most of which were on the Muslim woman and her duties. There was also a complete recording of the Quran, as well as its exegesis, some prayers, and various sayings of the Prophet.

I never really felt busy, or that the housework took up all my time. But then, I never seemed to have any free time either – it was as though even the void that might have filled my days was missing.

Walls are walls, but being cut off from my studies was like being cut off from life. Was I bored? I kept asking myself this, but I wasn't sure how people got bored or what they felt like when they were. If I had been bored, or felt something like boredom, then maybe I would have done something about it. I felt that I was nothing, and that the things around me were nothing too.

★

I finally found an opportunity to put Lula's advice into practice. She said it was guaranteed to give me a taste of the zeet-meet. That night, as soon as Abu Abdullah had finished reciting the optional *tajahud* prayer, as he did each night an hour before bed, he dropped to his knees, sobbing, and called on God to make the Muslims victorious. Before marrying him I'd never seen anyone pray like this.

Every night he would address God as though debriefing Him on the latest events in Afghanistan, Pakistan, Chechnya, Somalia and Palestine. Abu Abdullah would ask God to make His Muslim servants victorious against the infidels. I used to wish he'd also ask God to give him the vigour and vitality for married life, but he never did.

Eventually, I came to know his prayers by heart. So that night, even though his sobs muffled his words, I knew what he was saying: 'O Lord, have mercy on your servants, and save them from the fires of the infidels, from the oppression of the misguided people. Bring victory against the infidels to your servants in Peshwar, Tora Bora . . . O Lord, kill the Christians and the Jews. Do not allow them to overcome us. O Lord, uproot them and send flocks of the fierce Ababil birds against them. Defeat them with your unseen soldiers. Overcome them with the army of Islam, the army of Muhammad, the army of mujahideen who fight in your cause . . . O Almighty God! O Most Strong! O Protector! O Supreme in Greatness! O Avenger! O Subduer! O Most Great. My Lord, annihilate them, leave none of them standing! O God . . . O God . . . O God . . . O Answerer of prayers . . . O Defender of your servants . . . O Lord . . . O Lord, answer my prayers . . . O God . . . O Lord of the Mighty Throne.'

He was all pleading, his voice quavering and choked by his sobbing. I'd never been in a position to take the initiative before. I thought about trying to comfort him; stroking or holding him, arousing him so that things would go the way Lula believed they would – zeet-meet. I reached out my hand to quietly uncap the bottle of special perfume and splashed most of it over my neck and breasts, and under my arms. Then I slipped out of bed and stood behind him, stroking the back of his bowed head: 'What's wrong, darling? God will make them victorious. He is the All-Hearing, the All-Answering. He will lead His servants in Afghanistan to victory. He won't let them down. He's the All-Powerful. Come, darling. Come, sit up. Take heart. Come to bed. Come, my man, my prince, my dear. Come my king in this world. Lie beside me and hold me. Forget your worries and show me what you can do. Unsheathe your sword. Come. Get up.'

I led him to the bed, but the only words he seemed to have heard were 'lie beside me.'

The perfume bottle remained open until the following night at around the same time, when Abu Abdullah had finished his prayers and supplications. He seemed less worked up, more composed than he had been the previous night.

'Tomorrow I'm taking you to the home of the group's deputy chief. You'll be introduced to his wife. She's going to prepare you to become a defender of your faith and bring you closer to God.' I didn't say anything. I noticed my hand had reached out automatically to put the cap back on the perfume bottle.

★

As soon as we got to the deputy chief's house Abu Abdullah
directed me to a door on the ground floor – or what he
called the harem's wing. I knocked on the door while
he climbed an iron ladder to the upper level. When the
guard at the main gate had seen me with Abu Abdullah
he had averted his eyes, but the girl who opened the door
to the harem's wing just stared at me, until I thought there
must be something odd about my appearance.

Her body, including her eyes, were enveloped in a long
veil and a black abaya, so when she'd opened the door I
hadn't been able to make out a thing.

It was only after she had closed the door and moved
her veil aside that I saw she was just a girl, who couldn't
have been more than eleven years old. I showed her my
face, in turn, and said to her, 'Call your mother for me and
tell her that Abu Abdullah's wife is here.'

'Umm al-Mujahid, you mean. I'll go and speak to her.'
She came back and asked me to wait while Umm
al-Mujahid finished her meeting with the harem.

Over half an hour later there was a knock at the door
at the far end of the room. The girl asked me to cover my
face, then two women emerged. Neither of them acknowledged me in any way as they left – not even so much as
a 'salam.'

I was struck by the heavy scent of perfume emanating
from the far corner of the room where Umm al-Mujahid
– as I'd now began to think of her – was sitting.

I thought it odd that the sheikha's face was still veiled,
so I removed mine to encourage her to do the same.

'Do you reveal your face so easily? How, in the name
of God, will you make jihad with us? We're living in an
ignorant, infidel society. We must fight it with weapons and

strength. Our strength is in abiding by the true teachings of our sacred law.'

I was embarrassed and didn't know how to explain myself.

'I felt myself drawn to you right away. I felt I could trust you, like you were my mother, so I took off my veil.' She raised a finger in warning as though to pin down the last words she'd heard. Then she said: 'Nowadays money, children, father, mother, sister, brother have no value, so don't trust anyone in your family or your close friends – not even your mother. Put your trust, all of it, in God, may He be exalted.'

Hearing her speak like this, I was sure I'd never be able to keep up with her in a debate. I decided to keep quiet, to just listen and do what I was told. Abu Abdullah hadn't warned me of this. At school, back when I was still mastering the alphabet, I learnt that there are three kinds of obedience: obedience to God, obedience to His Prophet and obedience to your parents. After I married these became just two: obedience to God and obedience to your husband. But in truth, there is only one, since to obey your husband is to obey God. I pulled my veil back over my face and tried to tried to find the right words to convey my obedience: 'Thank you, may God grant you good health. I . . . I seek only God's approval. I've come to you for guidance, to help me fight in defence of God's religion.'

My words seemed to please her. She quizzed me on every aspect of my life: family, friends, relationships, childhood, studies, hobbies, desires. She even asked me if I'd ever taken a liking to one of my cousins or the young men in the neighbourhood and wanted to marry any of them.

Side A of the song

Ask my heart . . .

Ask my heart when it repents
Perhaps it will hold beauty to blame.

I began to visit Umm al-Mujahid regularly. I never once saw her face, although she'd always make sure she looked at mine to check it was really me under the veil and abaya. 'You are to go to the library every day between 8 and 10 am. You will spend this time in the newspaper archive, reading the papers that print articles offensive to the faith. Make a note of the authors' names and the subjects of their articles. If you believe a writer has violated sharia, especially if he's written about what they call 'women's freedom,' write his name down separately and make a summary of the article and the offending opinions.' This was my first assignment from Sheikha Umm al-Mujahid.

One day I was so absorbed in what I was reading that I ended up staying in the library an hour longer than I was supposed to. When I told Umm al-Mujahid, she was furious. It was only then that I learnt why she'd been so specific about the hours I should spend there: 'After ten there are a lot more library staff – since they usually arrive late – which means there are more people curious about your reading the papers and . . . and, do not forget, above all else, your main role as a hurma is to stay at home. You need to be home in time to make your husband's lunch.'

Ask a sensible man for sensible answers
But who could keep his wits in the face of such beauty?

I was reluctant to show Umm al-Mujahid my initial findings. It didn't seem reasonable to tell her or write in my report that most of the writers whose articles I'd read violated sharia in some way or another. This would mean the Prophet was wrong when he said 'Faith and Wisdom are Yemeni.'

I noticed that a bearded man with an extremely religious look about him would arrive at the library around the same time as me. He'd read through the same volumes I'd already read or the ones I'd earmarked to read later. I was scared he was watching me, or that he'd been sent to vet my work. I wasn't sure how to write my report. Could I keep back some of the names and articles of the writers who I believed were well intentioned and hadn't meant to violate sharia? But what if the bearded man's assignment was the same as mine, and if in the end someone was going to compare what we'd written?

I needed to find some excuse to talk to him, to get to know him a little. But just the thought of it made me feel worse. How should I behave with this person? What if he thought that whatever I might say to him was irreligious, more so than the stuff we'd both been reading? I mulled it over for a while, but there was no escaping it, I had to speak to him. The pretext I came up with was terrible but effective. He sat at a table jotting down his observations on lined paper, stacks of bound newspaper volumes piled high around him. I just had to take that first step, follow it with a few more, and then I'd be standing directly in front of him.

'Peace be upon you and God's mercy and blessings, brother in the eyes of God.'

He looked up at me and then quickly lowered his eyes.

'Peace be upon you and God's mercy and blessings,' he replied in a low, cracked voice that betrayed his embarrassment.

'God preserve you brother. I just wanted to ask you if you have a sister named Fatima? She entrusted me with something important about a year ago, at university, but I haven't seen her since. I've heard she died and also that she married and moved away. God forgive me, but to be honest when I saw your face I noticed you look at lot like her. I'm a God-fearing Muslim woman and avoid looking at men's faces, but I felt that God the High and Almighty had caused my gaze to fall on you. I don't believe God would deceive a faithful servant trying to fulfil an old promise.'

I'd spent some time practicing these words in my head until I knew them off by heart. I hadn't really been predicting how he might respond, but I don't think I could have ever anticipated anything like the reply he gave: 'Yes, Fatima is my sister. God have mercy on her soul. She died not long after starting university.'

'Oh, really? No, that can't be,' I said, embarrassed, not because his sister had actually died, but because I was surprised he'd even had a sister called Fatima in the first place. Not only that, she had even attended the same university as me, at the same time, and died before she could finish her first year, or suddenly disappeared, just as my story had it.

'I'm shocked. I can't believe it. God have mercy on her soul. I can't talk about this right now but, God willing, maybe we can talk again some other time. God preserve you, good bye.'

He didn't reply, just mumbled something I couldn't make out. Perhaps he was choking back the tears after I'd reminded him of his dead sister.

If I were to ask my heart
Tears would answer in its place.

I never had a friend called Fatima who died or suddenly disappeared during my first year at university. I began to wonder if I had a bad memory, but no one just forgets like that. Perhaps she was only at university for a few days before she died. After a lot of thought, I said to Fatima's brother: 'The dearly departed asked me to deliver something very important to someone. That person then entrusted me with something to deliver to Fatima. True, it's very precious and valuable, but it's not an actual thing. It's more a message she was supposed to hear from me, but now she's gone I can't speak of it to anyone else, God have mercy on her soul. I will take the secret of what this person said to the grave.'

He nodded his head in understanding and I felt myself relax – although this only lasted a few moments, before he asked, 'Why are you looking at the papers? Are you a student or a researcher?' A few seconds went by, as I watched him pick up another volume and leaf through it, until I said, 'I'm a student. But I read the papers to benefit from them, not for research. And you, are you a researcher?'

'The papers are no good. They're full of falsehood and slander. I'm a master's student at the college of Islamic law in Sana'a University. My supervisor asked me to do some research. My first task is to look at the cultural leanings of writers and journalists and how far they conform with or go against sharia.'

Reassured, I slowly began to sum up my report, passing over some violations of sharia where this seemed unintentional.

In my chest there is only flesh and blood
Feeble now that youth has gone.

Once, when I came to see the sheikha, I was surprised to find six other women there. They sat around the room on cushions, their hair and faces bare, dressed in short and flimsy clothes that barely covered their thighs and cleavages. Two of them were dressed differently to the others – one wore a skirt that reached to just below the knees, and the other a long sheer nightie that covered her shoulders and reached down to her ankles. After I'd greeted them, the sheikha asked me to take off my abaya, veil and headscarf, and hang them next to those of the other women. I was very embarrassed, since the clothes I was wearing underneath weren't exactly anything to write home about, and they weren't that clean either. I had on the same blouse I'd worn that morning when I cooked breakfast, and I'd worn the same trousers for three days in a row.

But why such a wanton display, when the sheikha had got so furious with me for simply taking my veil off, that time? And why didn't she do as the others did, or at least remove her veil?

'That's enough for today. God willing, we'll continue the lesson tomorrow,' said the sheikha, gesturing for them to leave without waiting for me to sit down – a relief, since I was afraid of what she might ask from me with them still in the room.

After they'd left, I handed her my report. I'd spent five days at home preparing it. It wasn't all that long, but my reticence had slowed me down. While her eyes were glued to the report, I took a good look at the objects scattered around her and beside an open metal trunk. It was about a metre and a half in length and three quarters of a metre wide. The objects had most likely come out of the trunk. There was an assortment of small stubby perfume bottles, various make-up accessories, and pointed tubes that I couldn't identify. I also noticed a white electric lamp, long and thin. A thought flashed into my mind as though the lamp had zapped me with an electrical charge: Were these objects supposed to resemble a man's thing? What did this have to do with these women and their lesson from the sheikha? 'Oh! I can't stop thinking about it because I'm not getting any,' I told myself as the little girl entered the room. She put the things back in the trunk, closed it and dragged it through a door into another room I hadn't noticed before. The door had been skilfully decorated over, so that its edges blended perfectly into the wall and it became invisible.

The sheikha berated the girl for not putting the trunk away quickly enough, then turned her attention to me.

'What's this! Just five writers? Only five writers who have violated sharia? Did you actually read anything? Did

you bother to look properly, or is it just that you don't
know anything about sharia in the first place?'

'I looked carefully, Miss— I mean, Sheikha. That's all
there was. After all, we are in the country of faith and
wisdom as the Prophet described it – peace be upon him.'

I could tell from the way she was still shaking her head
that she was fuming. 'You're ignorant. The Prophet, peace
be upon him, was talking about the Yemenis of old, the
faithful, not the infidels of these times, the end of time.
Haven't you heard what the Prophet said about the end of
time? He said that for those who hold onto their faith it
will be like holding hot coals.'

'Yes, yes. I know it off by heart.'

She didn't give me the chance to explain myself further.
Pulling a bunch of papers out from beneath the rug she
was sitting on, she said, 'Here, look at this report on the
infidel writers. Look how detailed it is.'

She didn't actually hand me the report but I could make
out some of the words on the front page. At the top of the
page, scrawled in spidery handwriting, was 'Mujahideen
Affairs Division: For information and action.' Below this was
a printed letter, which I noticed was addressed to an official
at the Political Security Bureau, though I couldn't make out
the name. It began: 'This study is per your request. We
commissioned brother Abu Misaab to undertake it.' I skimmed
to the bottom of the letter and saw it was signed by a Dr
Abu Jihad, described as a professor at Sana'a University.

Could it be that Abu Misaab was the masters student
I'd met at the library? This was the name he'd given, but
he hadn't told me the name of his professor. Was Abu Jihad
a codename, or a secret organisational name under which
he worked for military intelligence?

The sheikha seemed to be waiting for me to say something.

'Look! Look at the detail! The name of every writer and journalist who has violated the sharia is recorded here, with a summary and excerpts of what they've written. Look! Look at this!' she said. She turned back the first page and I was astonished by what I saw. It was the same handwriting that, when I'd first seen it, had seemed totally unique. It was Abu Misaab's writing, which resembled the ancient style of calligraphy they used to write the Quran in.

Was the professor working alone for military intelligence? If so, had he given Abu Misaab this assignment without telling him it was part of an intelligence operation? Or was Abu Misaab working for military intelligence too? The professor mentions in the letter that he assigned it to Abu Misaab, so did this mean they were familiar with him? But if they were, did this necessarily mean he was working with them? If either or both of them were working for military intelligence, then how had the report reached the sheikha? Was one of them working for military intelligence and the jihadi group? Or was it that military intelligence itself was working for both sides, copying its reports for the jihadi group to provoke them against the writers they considered infidels?

'What's to be done now? What should I do with you? What do you think the solution is?' said the sheikha.

The sheikha seemed very agitated. She kept moving her hands about, making it impossible for me to read what was written on the page.

'The decision is in God's hands. My work is whatever God guides you to,' I said to her, beginning to feel that this might well be the last time I saw her.

My heart weeps and I say: It's over
In my chest it trembles and I say: Repent!

A week went by during which I didn't once visit the sheikha.
Every morning, Abu Abdullah got up early and went to
the mosque to pray the dawn prayer, though he wouldn't
return until after the evening prayer. I asked him over and
over again why by the time he came home he was always
so exhausted and covered in dirt. Eventually he answered
'We're preparing for jihad in the cause of God.' Then he
added 'The hurma of the sheikh, the deputy chief, requests
that you go to see her tomorrow.'

Even if hearts were made of iron
Still none could bear what mine has suffered.

Umm al-Mujahid told me that this time my assignment
would be an easy one. All I had to do was visit the homes
of some of the families who lived in my neighbourhood.
I was to attend their celebrations, births and funerals and
then describe my observations in a detailed report.

'If you can even get into the bedrooms, then do. Write
down everything you see – perfume brands, make-up,
nightclothes . . . What do they watch on television? What
videos do they own? What do they read? What are the
names of the schools their children go to? What kind of
clothes do they wear? What do they eat? What do they
drink? How do they greet one another: peace be upon
you and God's blessings and mercy, or just peace be upon
you, or do they say Good evening, and Good morning?'
She gave me a small video camera with which I was to
record every detail.

At first, some things seemed unimportant. For example, if a person said 'Good morning' then I'd know he didn't adhere to the formal Islamic greeting, 'Peace be upon you and God's blessings and mercy.' And since he didn't adhere to the Islamic greeting, it was safe to assume he didn't adhere to all the principles of sharia. But after a while, Umm al-Mujahid revealed how even the seemingly insignificant things mattered.

'Simple facts aren't enough. A God-fearing sister might use a deodorant bottle shaped like a penis to masturbate because she is scared she will not be able to control her desire and commit the sin of adultery. Another hurma might use a deodorant bottle to masturbate because her husband no longer desires her, which means she might cheat on him if she isn't committed to sharia. We learn about the nature of the relationship between the hurma and her husband and how we might influence them, to guide them to Islam, or at least one of them or their children. We encourage them to combat manifestations of disbelief in the home.'

I found it difficult. Actually, I was really uncomfortable trying to get close to these families without any real pretext. But despite my unease, I got on with it. I was convinced that it was a duty in my jihad, my struggle in God's cause – the cause of implementing the righteous sharia.

I did this for two months, going from one home to the next. As the sheikha had instructed, I focussed on intellectuals and other prominent members of the community. Eventually I got to know the family of a minister who was close to the president. The sheikha asked me to provide her with detailed information on the family, and how to contact its members.

I did as I was asked. The sheikha introduced me to a young girl and asked me to fill her in. Then she told me to introduce her to the family as my sister. I didn't know why the sheikha felt it was time for me to take a step back and make room for this person presented as my sister to take over.

No one can tell you about life's hardships
Like someone who has lost their loved ones.

Her decision surprised me, but it seemed to make more sense than me continuing to spy on the families. That day, Abu Abdullah was irate as he took me to have my photo taken for a new passport. 'We'll go to Afghanistan to fight with the mujahideen. We'll stand with them against the infidel crusaders. Then we'll come back and fight this infidel state that makes women and men have their photos taken for passports and identity cards, when it is forbidden by sharia!'

When I went to visit my parents I learnt that 'Abd al-Raqeeb had beaten us to the front. He'd chosen Chechnya as his destination for jihād, fighting with the Muslims against the Russian communists.

Those who are dazzled by the riches of this world
Should know that I wore its finery until it fell to rags.

We got visas for Saudi Arabia. I didn't really understand why they were for Saudi and not Afghanistan, but as a hurma it wasn't my place to ask. This was men's business, after all. Abu Abdullah said that Riyadh was to be our first stop on the road to Afghanistan.

We stayed four days in Riyadh. While we were there we got to know some Saudi families. The women would come to visit me at the villa we were staying in. On the first day, five of them arrived after the afternoon prayer. Umm Muhammad, as she called herself, made the introductions: 'We are all from the harem of the mujahideen who have gone to Afghanistan. Only Umm al-Qaqa's husband is still here,' she said, pointing to a very elegant young woman whose strikingly beautiful face wore a look of joy tempered by anxiety. 'God bless her, she's insisted he takes her with him to jihad. They're newly-weds,' she added with a smile.

The women's frequent visits to the villa over the following days bestowed many gifts on me. Once Umm Muhammad brought along her daughter, who couldn't have been more than seventeen years old. She sat without saying a word, expressionless – except once, when I noticed a sarcastic smile play across her lips while her mother was talking. When we got up to say the sunset prayer, the young girl stood next to me. I saw that she wasn't really paying much attention to the prayer. I didn't say anything, even when she failed to end her prayer properly by turning her head to the right.

They spent most of the time discussing some recent fatwas that were being hotly debated in all the papers. These fatwas concerned the ban on women drivers, and whether it was permissible for a woman to make a male colleague become her kin – and therefore conform to sharia – by breastfeeding him.

The women often said things like: 'We are the harem . . . It's the harem's duty . . . God created the harem to . . . Come on, harem . . . I'm the hurma of a mujahid . . .'

I realised that Abu Abdullah's habit of using the word 'harem' to mean 'women' was probably a legacy of the nine years he'd spent in Saudi Arabia. He told me he had been just thirteen years old when he arrived. The family had begged a relative to put Abu Abdullah on his passport as his son, so he could work and earn money in Saudi. Despite his youth Abu Abdullah had begun work in a clothes shop as soon as he arrived, and continued until his return to Yemen at twenty-three, on assignment from a jihadi group. A few weeks after his return he began to distance himself from his family. They'd ignored his call to 'abandon their sinful ways,' as he put it. That was when he married me, after he'd got to know 'Abd al-Raqeeb.

During our stay at the villa, a lovely Indian girl called Andeera looked after me, keeping me company for much of the time I was in Riyadh, except during the small hours when Abu Abdullah was at home. She told me she'd become a Muslim two years before. I took the opportunity to ask her what she knew about Hindus worshipping cows and other animals.

She spoke openly, as though my question had made her happy, or she was relishing the opportunity to think about this subject. She said the cow was a sacred religious symbol and that there were many stories around it. In broken Arabic with the odd English word thrown in, she explained how Hindus considered every living thing to be sacred.

I don't remember everything she said, except that she'd learned from her husband that true faith is to emulate God's ways: 'We must emulate God in our behaviour, but not in fear of punishment or in expectation of reward. If we obey His instructions because we expect to be rewarded, or because we fear His punishment, then we have not attained true faith.'

I saw in her eyes a longing for the past, or perhaps her family. Her words moved me, and they stayed with me, so that I woke up with them still in my head: 'If we obey His instructions because we expect to be rewarded, or because we fear His punishment, then we have attained true faith.'

'I seek refuge in God!' I said, to protect myself from the effect of her blasphemous words, but instantly regretted it – although I'd only muttered the Islamic incantation I couldn't help thinking Andeera might have heard. Trying to shake off her influence on me, I said outloud 'They're infidels, they're ignorant, they're heathens, they're . . .' I frowned at myself in the mirror, trying to look like someone else, someone intolerant towards anything that contradicted the creed of monotheism, but just then Andeera knocked on the door. She came in with her gentle smile, as though she were every mother, every child and every sweet Indian cow.

From its gardens I gathered roses and thorns
And from its cup I tasted honey and resin.

The day before we left Riyadh Andeera went off somewhere with one of the women visitors, who'd gestured for Andeera to follow her.

I was alone except for the television, which you could have called an Islamic television, since it showed only channels that specialised in Quran – recitation, exegesis, fatwas and the Muslim family.

I flicked through the channels for a while and then went to say the sunset prayer. After I came back, I found myself glued to a Muslim women's show that was debating the notorious breastfeeding fatwa issued by an Egyptian sheikh. The sheikh, I forget his name, was a department head at Cairo's famous al-Azhar university. The presenter said the sheikh had ruled that if a woman must, for some unavoidable reason, spend time in the presence of a man who is neither her husband nor a close relative – which is of course pro-hibited by sharia – then it's possible for her to suckle this man, thereby creating a kinship bond between them and making it permissible for them to mix. Sheikha Umm al-Qawasim, who sat next to the presenter, was very enthu-siastic about the fatwa. She said the ruling was based on something the Prophet, peace be upon him, had said when one of his companions, Suhla Bint Suhail, came to him and complained about how her husband, Abu Hadhiqa, didn't like the servant greeting her, since he had now reached manhood. The Prophet instructed her to breastfeed the servant and make him family.

The programme was being broadcast live, and invited its female viewers to call in with their questions and comments. Was this one of those encoded channels, only for women, that I'd heard of? I'd been able to watch it without entering a password so perhaps whoever took care of the house had left it like that. When Abu Abdullah had left, the television was playing a Quran recitation, but Andeera showed me how to change the channels.

I was surprised by the bluntness of some of the viewers' questions. If they hadn't cited verses from the Quran and the words of the Prophet – peace be upon him – I might have doubted their Islam. One viewer said in astonishment: 'God bless our venerable sheikh who has shown us that sharia can solve any problem, including the mixing of the two sexes.' The second caller agreed with the first and said she would breastfeed her male colleagues the next day, so she could mix with them without feeling sinful, something that had been really bothering her.

One of the callers thought the fatwa was wonderful but wondered how she could suckle the family's Ethiopian driver and make him family, given that he was Christian?

Sheikha Umma al-Qawasim's voice betrayed her confusion and she continued to skirt around the question, even though she'd answered all the previous questions with the conviction of someone who believed she spoke with the authority of God's law.

Still, anyone would have thought from the presenter's emphatic nodding that the sheikha was giving the viewer a definitive answer. The presenter cut the sheikha short and moved on to the next caller, who introduced herself as Umm Maadh. The new caller didn't allow the sheikha or the presenter to worm their way out of answering her question. Instead, she dragged them, along with the rest of the viewers, into a maze of questions that had no answers: Should a woman suckle a man directly from her breasts, or should she express the milk and offer it to him in a receptacle of some kind? Doesn't the fatwa use the word 'breastfeed,' and not 'give a drink to' or 'quench the thirst of'? How was this done in the Prophet's day? If a woman is unmarried or not lactating then what does she do?

Amid the dark folds of their abayas, all that was visible of the sheikha and presenter were four glints of light, indicating the eye-slits of their veils. Even so, their voices boomed out loud and clear, while the camera darted from one angle to another.

The presenter decided to take some more calls before answering the last caller's questions, asking the sheikha – she seemed very eager to reply – to answer them all together. This actually worked out better in the end, since there were some great questions: Is it permitted for a woman to shake the hand of a man she has breasfed? If a woman takes a taxi every day, not having a car of her own, should she suckle the driver every day? How many times does a man have to be breastfed? Is it possible to use a breast pump and feed him indirectly? If a man sucks his wife's nipples and ends up swallowing some of her milk, does this mean he's now like a son to her and their relationship becomes forbidden? If a woman is alone with a man she has suckled, then how does she deal with the religious police if they find them together?

The sheikha's answers were arbitrary and unconvincing. It was obvious to me she wasn't sufficiently well versed in the subject, despite the confident tone with which she delivered her religious judgements (even if it was difficult to consider them at all valid). The debate became particularly heated after two callers announced their absolute rejection of the fatwa, describing it as an insult to Islam. Only one other caller agreed with them. She said the fatwa was like one of those inauthentic sayings attributed to the Prophet which contradicted the Quran, and that al-Azhar University had sacked the sheikh who issued it.

The sheikha declined to respond to one caller's obvious sarcasm: 'I followed the fatwa – I asked the driver into the house so that I could breastfeed him. I gave him one of my breasts to suck on, and he kept sucking and sucking but no milk came out. So I gave him the other one, and he sucked on it for even longer than the first – but there still wasn't any milk flowing. The good driver looked up and suggested he should try licking other parts of my body since this might stimulate it into activity and make it lactate. He got what he wanted, and milk began to pour from all my orifices, but not from my breasts. The driver lapped up the milk until he had his fill, and now he comes inside the house whenever he likes.'

The debate remained heated and I didn't think it was about to end any time soon, even though it had already been going on for an hour and a half. Before the sheikha had finished what she was saying, a key turned in the front door and Abu Abdullah came in. I noticed straight away that he was dressed differently from when he'd left the house that morning, but before I could ask him why he'd changed his clothes he told me – with an odd smile on his face – to close my eyes. I'd never seen him smile before or, for that matter, show any other discernible sign of happiness.

I closed my eyes and recalled a similar scene in an American movie I'd watched at my aunt's house when I was a girl: a man asks a woman to sit beside him and close her eyes. Then he pulls a present from his pocket and says 'Open you eyes.' He surprises her with a pearl necklace. It has a triangular pendant, perhaps white gold, engraved with 'You are my heart's desire.' I sensed Abu Abdullah move back towards the front door, which he'd left ajar. 'Open your eyes to see the surprise!'

He was right about it being a surprise. I didn't just open my two eyes – a million eyes all over my body sprang wide open when I found a woman before me wearing an amazing wedding dress like nothing I'd ever seen before. I was speechless. For a moment I didn't understand. At first, I thought she was some sort of bridal doll made from flesh and blood, an extraordinary doll, an example of the latest fashion in the world of dolls. I stumbled and swayed while my eyes, all the eyes in my body, remained wide open, fixed on my first ever present from Abu Abdullah.

'It's Andeera . . . Andeera!' I said to myself, her identity dawning on me as I examined the familiar features of the woman who appeared clearly from behind the thin white veil that hung over her face.

At first, I couldn't understand what was going on. I felt so confused that I distracted myself by rearranging some of the cushions in the sitting room. I can remember the moment vividly; it was as though I were just going about the household chores, plumping up the cushions and smacking the dust off them. It was exactly as Mother used to do, except that the cushions in Riyadh weren't dusty. When I suddenly grasped what was happening, my whole body went rigid with rage. I automatically reached for him but quickly checked myself. I didn't want to just slap him, I wanted to totally destroy him, like that bomb that exploded in an American movie I once saw. My body, my whole body was like a bomb he'd lit the fuse of – it was about to blow him to smithereens along with his gift. I never thought that a bomb could be stopped once the fuse was lit. But that is exactly what happened, when Andeera placed her hand on my shoulder and her smile widened in that way I was now so familiar with. My muscles relaxed and I suddenly felt drained of every ounce of strength. I didn't have to relinquish the marital bed to my husband's new bride – as is expected from a woman who obeys God's law, which gives a man the right to marry four women – as another bedroom had already been made up.

★

When the call to prayer sounded from the nearby mosques, Abu Abdullah went to the mosque next door to the villa to pray with the congregation. I made my ablutions and waited for Andeera to come out of the other bathroom so that we could pray together.

I didn't sleep that whole night: I was kept awake by pangs of jealousy. I tried to listen in on them but I couldn't hear a thing, not even a whisper. I kept asking myself, 'What am I so jealous of?' But I only had to imagine the two of them lying next to each other in bed for the anger to bubble up once more.

'May God make your happiness continue,' I said to the bride as she walked towards me.

Andeera always looked happy or had a smile on her face, even if this wasn't obvious from her lips. There are no words to describe the sheer delight she exuded – she was simply a ball of joy.

I wanted to ask her how her night had been, but I didn't dare.

Andeera and I sat next to each other on the plane, while Abu Abdullah sat to the right of us on the other side of the aisle. I discovered that all our travel documents had been produced in Riyadh with new Saudi names and identities instead of our real ones, including Andeera's name, which was now Aisha al-Ghamidi. We weren't exactly scrutinised on our way through passport control.

As we left the villa in Riyadh, I felt like I was literally covered from head to foot in the gold Abu Abdullah had brought: bracelets, anklets, pendants, chains, necklaces, heavy rings on every finger, a watch, a tiara, belts – all very weighty and expensive. I was weighed down by gold, as though it were a heavy dress.

It looked like Andeera was wearing just as much gold as I was, since it covered most of her body. The two suitcases that had been checked in under her name were filled with make-up compacts and an assortment of perfume bottles. I couldn't see any difference between them and the two suitcases that Abu Abdullah had checked in under my name, except for their orange and brown colour scheme. They weighed roughly the same. Each of us had her personal luggage, although Abu Abdullah showed no interest in these like he did the four suitcases.

I was happy when I first put on the gold and saw the perfume and make-up, but I soon felt differently when I realised that gold and make-up don't go with jihad. These things belong to a beautiful woman, the hurma at home. 'What's the problem? True, I'm a jihadi, but I'm also a hurma and I should make myself pretty,' I told myself, after giving it some thought.

Abu Abdullah insisted I wear all the gold, but he warned me not to open any of the perfume bottles or the make-up. There was a kohl pot, which looked old and worn. Pointing to it, he said, 'Be warned.'

'Marriage is wonderful, don't you think?' I said to Andeera as the plane prepared for take-off.

'Wonderful, wonderful. Marriage is wonderful,' she said.

I tried to make my meaning clearer: 'Marriage . . . Marriage is wonderful. You are the wife. You are the wife, the hurma. He is the husband, the man. You understand. Marriage is two people together. Hurma and man in one marriage. Understand?'

'Means that . . . that man and hurma, he husband together, together,' she said with a giggle and then added, her laughter growing louder, 'It's all zig-zig. Man and hurma together. All zig-zig.'

'What's zig-zig? I don't understand.'

She giggled again at my question.

'You don't understand? No, not possible. You zig-zig. Doesn't make sense,' she said, thrusting her index finger in and out of a loose fist.

'Aha, zig-zig is zeet-meet,' I said, remembering Lula's explanation of the same act.

'Zig-zig. I don't understand zeet-meet,' she said, and tried to explain it in words she thought I might understand: 'You and Abu Abdullah. You and he together make zig-zig.' Again, she made the same gesture with her finger and fist. I was fairly certain I understood what she meant but she was convinced I still hadn't got it.

'You understand. Abu Abdullah come you and zig-zig. You like this wife. You understand?'

This was my opportunity to find out what had happened between them on their wedding night. 'How were you? Did Abu Abdullah bring zig-zig?'

'No Abu Abdullah no bring. Abu Abdullah no make zig-zig.'

I felt relief. There'd been no zig-zig between Abu Abdullah and Andeera, just like there'd been no zeet-meet between Abu Abdullah and I.

'What's this? Why didn't Abu Abdullah didn't bring zig-zig? That's not right,' I said.

'Why . . .Abu Abdullah bring you zig-zig?' she wondered in surprise, although I got the feeling she already understood the nature of the relationship between Abu Abdullah and I, just as she understood her relationship with me, even if only a night had passed since their wedding. She leaned her head back as though remembering something: 'You know, zig-zig not so important. You relax like this.'

'How can I relax – how can you – when there's no zig-zig?'

'You, I understand a lot. You tired. Me, no. I sleep. My husband comes zig-zig.'

'I don't understand. How can you sleep and Abu Abdullah bring zig-zig?'

'No, no. You don't understand. I sleep. Other husband bring zig-zig.'

'What, your second husband? Are you married to two men?'

'Other husband, me India. Other I love. I love him husband. I in Riyadh. In India I have husband in China. I sleep. My husband sleep together.'

'You mean, you meet your Indian husband in your dreams?'

'Dreams. You understand. Half dreams. Half sleep. Half no sleep.'

'Between dreams and waking. You mean fantasies. But this is serious. How can you be married to two men, Abu Abdullah and an Indian?'

'I am Muslim. I have four husbands.'

I laughed out loud and was sure everyone on the plane must have heard me. For a moment I thought Andeera didn't understand the sharia's position on marriage, but then I realised she was laughing too. Even so I was disturbed that, despite embracing Islam and marrying Abu Abdullah, she was still connected to her previous husband.

'I have Indian husband. Sheikh come yesterday. He

speak, say, India marriage not right. India husband infidel. You Muslim. You wife of Muslim. You and Abu Abdullah married together.'

I didn't know if it was permitted for her to marry a Muslim man if she was already married to a non-Muslim or an infidel, as the sheikh had said. I understood from Andeera that her Indian husband followed a philosophical path related to yogic meditation in India, and that their guru had sent him to China to spread their ideas there. She pulled out a small book that she said contained sacred Indian wisdom. I didn't understand her translation of some things, but I understood that they call for mastery of the senses, and teach that desire is an enemy of wisdom. They also call for liberation from binaries like pain and pleasure, love and hate, failure and success. All these things are equal and their source is the senses. We must avoid selfishness and work without coveting reward and personal gain or fear of punishment.

It wasn't just the message in what Andeera was saying that made me feel at ease; there was something about the way she spoke and the clarity of her voice – despite her broken Arabic – which I found very comforting. But what really left a deep impression on me was Andeera's appearance after we'd sat a while in silence. I noticed she was crying and trembling, almost as though writhing against invisible thorns. I imagined that as she cried with joy, she was witnessing a great miracle, as though God had appeared to her. As though she were close to Him, between His hands.

In Cairo, we stayed in a large house next door to our Egyptian host family. A gate in the wall between the two courtyards connected the properties. A little corridor ran between the gate and our front door. It was shaded by a trellis woven with flowers so that anyone looking down from the rooms above couldn't see who was passing though. About an hour after we arrived, Abu Abdullah went off somewhere with our host, who had picked us up from the airport. Andeera and I decided to get some rest, and I slumped down into a comfy chair in the lounge and snoozed. At the sound of a key turning in the door I awoke with a jolt. I'd locked it as well as the outer door, and had even slid the bolts across. The key stopped moving in the lock and my breathing calmed. I was about to doze off again when a door on the other side of the room suddenly swung open and I sat up with a start. A woman dressed in a long Egyptian robe stepped into the room. She greeted me with the formal Islamic greeting and I realised she was our host's wife. She'd come in this way because she was afraid someone might be watching the house and discover who was inside. She told me there were three doors and that I only knew two of them: the third was apparently her secret.

The fright I'd got from her sudden entrance left me feeling uneasy for the rest of our stay, and I never really had a sense of being in Cairo. I struggled to stay interested in conversation, the words of our host's wife passing right over me. It was only when she and Andeera would laugh out loud that I'd realise she'd told a joke. I'd humour her with a smile and nod my head to seem interested in what she was saying.

I came to realise that our stop in Riyadh had been in order for us to receive instructions from some jihadi leadership or its supporters, and that we were to convey them to the mujahideen in Afghanistan. More importantly though, as I would realise later, we were to transport money and other items to them – the idea being that Abu Abdullah and I wouldn't arouse suspicion.

During the week we spent in Cairo, Abu Abdullah kept the keys to our luggage safe. Over the seven days we were there he repeatedly opened the suitcases, each time taking out a few of my make-up compacts and perfume bottles. I was mystified by his sudden interest in my perfume and make-up, and I had no idea where he was taking them.

But no wiser judgment than God's have I witnessed
And no door other than His have I sought.

In Sudan, it all seemed to make sense. In Riyadh and Cairo, I'd only really had a vague idea of our purpose, but in Khartoum I felt like I was actually a member of the team. Abu Abdullah told me he would be in constant training throughout the ten days we were to spend there, and that the Sudanese harem would take me to train with them separately every day, too. But Andeera wouldn't be joining me.

Abu Abdullah opened the suitcases only once in Sudan to take out a compact and two bottles of perfume. 'Have you got another hurma? Did you marry her in secret? Do you bring her perfume and make-up?' I teased. 'Yes, I have another beloved,' he said solemnly. 'She is the first and the last. I love her and desire her above all else. She is martyrdom in God's cause.' 'God's blessings,' I responded. His words encouraged me, strengthening my own resolve for jihad.

I learned, from the women, how to make food from trees and shrubs during a siege, as well as some basic first aid, such as how to dress wounds and broken bones with

Islamic remedies: plants, spices and herbs – even camel and cow's urine. When I heard about the benefits of cow dung, I thought of Andeera, who Abu Abdullah had insisted remain in the house, for reasons known only to him. One of the women instructed me on sexual relations during jihad: 'In times of peace, it must be limited to once a week and even then one should be careful to avoid over-exertion. But in times of war, it is prohibited altogether because the man must save his stamina for the enemy, so that he stays strong and fired-up. Sex weakens a man and leaves him passive and peaceful.' Most of them wanted to go to jihad and considered me lucky. I learnt that there are very few female Arab mujahideen.

What left the deepest impression on me during the training sessions were the religious songs I learned from the women – they were so rousing! The women told me that female mujahideen can enter the battle behind the men and beat the drums, singing:

> 'The volunteers are like beautiful flowers
> The servants of God are heading for jihad.'

One of the songs addresses the troops in battle, calling on them to martyr themselves and enter Paradise, where they will encounter the houris – the beautiful maidens of Paradise that God has promised them. The women sing it as though they themselves were the houris:

> 'Oh soldiers of God . . . Oh soldiers of God
> We are the maidens of Paradise in the Gardens of God.'

One of my favourites was a light and catchy number:

'Victory comes to the brave
Rise for jihad.'

Or:

'I'm Islamic . . . I'm Islamic.'

I began to enthuse about the songs to Abu Abdullah, but he quickly shut me up. 'They are a prohibited innovation. It is not permitted for a woman to sing them or to mix with men in battle.' He went on to remind me that the Prophet tells us a woman's jihad is her obedience to her husband.

Side B of the song (replay)

From its gardens I gathered roses and thorns
And from its cup I tasted honey and resin.

By the time we reached Afghanistan I'd already begun to forget the hardships of the journey. For the first time in my life I was about to do something that actually mattered, something tangible that would make me feel like I existed.

Abu Abdullah had given us back our original passports in Pakistan, telling us the Saudi passports we'd travelled there on had served their purpose. Andeera noticed that the stamps in our passports suggested we'd travelled directly from Saudi Arabia to Pakistan, and we wondered what was going on.

Andeera and I were met by a couple of Afghani women who dressed us in traditional Afghani clothes. One of them accompanied us into Afghanistan, along with four other women we hadn't met before. They were wearing a lot of gold too, like we were. Together, we took a corner in the back of the truck. Most of the passengers were men, so we huddled together in our Afghani clothes, behind the suitcases and out of view of the seven men, who were indistinguishable – even Abu Abdullah – in their Afghani dress. I didn't recognise the names of any of the towns we passed through or stopped off at, but I'll never forget names like Peshwar, Kabul, Qandahar, and Tora Bora. The men spoke of these places throughout the journey, but we women had no idea if we'd actually reached them or if it was just talk.

They took us to a narrow mountain cave. We slept on worn blankets, barely visible in the dim glow of a small lamp. 'In the thick of jihad, the mujahideen hadn't found the time, not even one second, to clean its black-ened glass,' I murmured to myself in the dark. I tried to imagine what the morning would bring, and picture the role I might play. I couldn't sleep, even though I was exhausted from all the travelling. I imagined myself under a hail of rockets and gunfire, carrying an injured mujahid with the help of another sister. We lay him down in a tent, and then she rushes back to help others, while I remain by his side. I gently pull his lose cotton trousers down as he cries out in pain. I deftly put into practice the first aid I learnt in Sudan. Around me the women call me a mujahida, a female fighter in God's cause. I'm not just a hurma anymore, not just Abu Abdullah's hurma. No one calls me hurma anymore – as we treat the wounded we call out to each other by our actual names: Khawla, come here; Aisha, pass me that; Here you go, Zaynab; Give me that, would you, Khadija? Sumiyya, hand me— Hafsa, take a look at this wound. God bless you, our sister in jihad. Our mujahideen brothers are in peril, they're being martyred one after the other. Over here, Umm Misaab. Come forward, take up your weapons. The time for jihad has come. Fight the infidels!

'Come to prayer. Come to Prayer. Prayer is better than sleep . . .' the call to prayer rang out. I thought I was still dreaming, or perhaps I was having a waking dream, one that continued whether I was asleep or awake.

But no wiser judgment than God's have I witnessed
And no door other than His have I sought.

It was a terrifying day, bigger than a dream. It was a day of blood, fire and death; a day of rockets, when bombs dropped from planes and explosions froze us in our tracks, paralysed. What was this formidable power those Western crusaders possessed? Where is Your power, my Lord? Where are Your invisible soldiers? Will You protect Your mujahideen, and not forsake them?

I didn't know what to do. I felt useless. All my dreams were powerless in the face of such a terrifying force. Was it a divine force sent by God to test the mujahideen? God forbid that He would do such a thing to His servants.

Andeera tried to calm me down – or that's what it looked like: I couldn't hear anything other than the sounds of near-by explosions. Afterwards I was told that it had been a missile strike. My head, my whole body exploded with a thousand questions. My thoughts tortured me: How could all that power, all those high-tech deadly weapons be put in the hands of infidels, while the Muslims were so weak? Was it a reckoning for the Muslims because they had lapsed in their faith, lapsed in everything? Or was it a trial from God?

Several times a voice called out 'The women are to gather in the first tent to the south.' It sounded as though something special was expected to happen to the women at sunset, and darkness had already begun to set in.

Nothing in life is worthier than kindness
Its blessings outlive the giver.

We learnt we were to leave the battleground, but we didn't know where we were going. Andeera and I collected our suitcases from the wooden hut they'd been kept in, and I also took a small bag Abu Abdullah had given me. He'd been very clear that I must take good care of it and in that moment I didn't know what else to do with it, since he wasn't to hand.

We left the male mujahideen to their fate: a battle in which defeat – or what some thought was defeat – became a synonym for victory. Defeat, including death, was victory for them, because it meant martyrdom, dying for God's cause.

We were a group of women crammed into an old Land Rover, its driver speeding us to an unknown destination.

I was never able to fulfill my dream, whether in reverie or reality, since I spent barely a night and a day at the front. Apart from our group there'd been no other women there. I was told the rest of the women were in a place far from the frontline. Their husbands visited them when their commanders gave them leave. Only a few of the women ever went to the front to sleep with their husbands, and even then only when their husbands couldn't leave their posts. Most of the mujahideen didn't bring their wives to jihad. Some of them married Afghani or Pakistani women, or the daughters of Arab mujahideen who'd been here a long time with their families. I learnt from the other women that we, Andeera and I, were only ever meant to stay there one night. Once the gold was collected from us and the suitcases full of make-up and perfume were handed over to the position's commander, all of us women were to go on to a nearby town where the harem were gathered. This confirmed my suspicions. The gold jewellery I'd carried on me had obviously been sent by supporters of the mujahideen to finance their activities, and the make-up compacts and perfume bottles contained materials needed by the mujahideen to make weapons to use against the infidels.

The aerial bombardment meant we couldn't take the direct route to where the rest of the harem where, but had to go on a long detour through the mountains.

A couple of hours into our night journey we came to a sudden stop. The blinding glare of flashlights flooded the car. Six men approached us, dressed in military uniforms decorated with an insignia I didn't recognise. They examined us by the light of their torches, exchanging words in a language I didn't understand. Simultaneously, the rear doors and the back door were flung open. A woman was pulled out from each. The men led them away towards the boulder-strewn roadside, one of them yelling at the driver what must have been an order before disappearing with the women. The other three men remained where they were, silent and alert, guns at the ready. The driver looked Afghani but we didn't know if the troops were Afghani, Iranian, Pakistani or of some other nationality.

The soldiers returned the three women to the car, then they searched our belongings, snatching the jewellery from our necks, wrists and ears. The only thing spared was the bag Abu Abdullah had entrusted me with, which I'd hidden between my legs. I think it must have been too small for them to notice.

. The men told the driver to go. Back on the road, the way women who'd been taken were sobbing told us they'd been raped.

The little boy who was riding up front talked to the driver in an Afghani language. He turned to us and said in Arabic 'He says he's taking us across the border into Iran.'

Strangely, it was only after the incident on the roadside that we started talking. I was sitting in the middle row of seats, next to an Egyptian who was married to an African American mujahid, and a Moroccan who was the wife of a French mujahid. Andeera was in the back row, jammed in between a Kurdish woman and two other women who were also married to mujahideen. The oldest of them was a Syrian woman who had two children with her. One of them, a girl, kept climbing over the back of the seats onto our laps. She must have been around seven or eight years old – it was hard to tell as she wore an abaya, headscarf and veil. The other child, a boy of about ten, was sitting next to the driver.

The Syrian woman told me that when her husband, Abu Sadeeq, had wanted to marry a Saudi mujahid's daughter in Afghanistan, he'd had no choice but to divorce her – his first wife and mother of his two children – because Islam only permits four wives and he already had three others, one of whom lived with her in the same house in Afghanistan. The third wife lived at home with her mother and the fourth lived in Saudi.

She added that God had willed she marry an Algerian mujahid, a friend of her ex-husband. She saw this as a way of ensuring she'd always be close to her children.

Next to her, by the door, sat Abu Sadeeq's latest wife, a Saudi. She looked around seventeen years old.

Andeera sat across from the two of them, with the grumpy looking Kurdish woman beside her. When I asked her where she was from – Syria, Iran, Iraq, or Turkey – she answered me angrily 'From the Kurdish jinn.'

It had been a matter of pure chance. The soldiers had grabbed the three women at random, because they happened to be sitting next to the doors they opened. I was most concerned for the Egyptian woman because from the way she cried, I felt it had to be more than the rape. Looking back on it now, I realise that she was crying for the many rapes she had endured. This latest rape had broken something inside her. Instead of just adding to her store of silent pain, it had brought something to the surface.

The Moroccan woman beside me was silent. Before the rape she'd been reciting prayers in a low, melodious voice. Now the only sound she made was the odd painful sigh. Since the soldiers had brought her back, the Abu Sadeeq's young Saudi wife had been angrily repeating the same words over and over again: 'Infidels, infidels, enemies of God.' After a while she went quiet and I glanced round to see if she was OK. Her posture was one of deep relaxation, but her tense smile told a different story. It was as though her body had fallen into a deep sleep, but her mind was still wide awake.

We stopped for a break – I think the little Syrian boy needed to pee. When we were getting back into the car I went out of my way to take the seat by the door. I let the other two women get back in first.

'You envious or something?' asked Umm al-Izz, the

Egyptian, laughing. I forced a laugh to match hers but didn't know what to say.

'I can rest my head against the window and sleep here – you're always awake anyway,' I said to her.

'No problem, whatever you like,' she laughed again, then whispered, 'How are these soldiers so strong? Do they eat Hadramaut honey or something?' She seemed to have heard about Hadramaut honey's properties as an aphrodisiac – the same honey I'd once hoped would work its magic on Abu Abdullah. Her words pained me; how pathetic, I couldn't even get my share of rape. I asked God's forgiveness for these thoughts but I couldn't get them out of my head. I waited for the moment when a solider would open the car door and drag me somewhere out of sight. But what if he did it in front of everyone? It would be a scandal. No, not a scandal. Let him rape me in front of everyone. It wouldn't matter. It would be rape, without my consent and I would not be to blame for it.

I fell asleep with these thoughts playing on my mind. When a soldier's hand reached out and opened the door I felt like I was still dreaming. But when he asked me to get out with the others I thought I must be in a different kind of dream, a dream that was reality. At the time I understood the difference between the two dreams, but now I don't remember, or at least I don't understand anymore. The soldier, along with four others, searched every inch of the car. I waited for him to take me somewhere hidden from sight but he motioned for us to get back in. I was sure now that the dream had ended.

This second search somehow made the first more real, and back on the road our conversation turned to the rapes. As I listened to the women recount their experiences and discuss those of other women they knew, I became convinced that rape is a hateful thing. It is abuse, an act of violence committed for the pleasure of one party against another.

At that point, Andeera joined in. What she said completely shifted the tone of the conversation. In spite of her poor pronunciation and the way she mixed Arabic and English words, her meaning was clear: the body is like a constant chatter at which God and the devil take turns – and sometimes they both talk at the same time. God measures words with the conscious mind. His language is expressed in chaste and modest behviour; but the devil also enters the body, and talks through it in another way. This can be seen in the unabashed gaze or the hand that reaches for the erogenous zones, or even outbreaks of venereal disease. Two tongues speaking inside one body. Rape might satisfy the devil inside us, but it will crush a woman who devotes herself to God, cloud her judgement and make her ask too many questions. Those who talk about freedom have allowed the devil to chatter in their bodies. We must stand with God against the devil.

It seemed Andeera's words had ended the conversion, since no one else spoke after that. In my mind I saw the image of the pure devout woman who dies a virgin, who guards her chastity and saves her vagina for her husband, virtuous and devoted. But unspoken questions soon bombarded me from all sides: In the end, as a virgin, will I be one of the women of Paradise who God will give as compensation to his God-fearing worshippers? Or will God create other such women? Don't we, the obedient, worshipping women who guard our chastity, have any pleasure awaiting us in heaven like men do?

The Prophet of kindness showed the way
He led by example, guiding the people.

The driver said something to the little boy. He must have learned to speak that particular Afghani language during the time he'd spent in Afghanistan with his parents. He turned his head and said 'The driver says we're now in Iran.'

We were stopped at a border checkpoint where we were asked countless questions, and had to fill in a lot of forms. The boy and the driver had their work cut out. In the end, we had to wait almost four hours before we were finally allowed through.

After we crossed the border into Iran I lost track of events. Drifting in and out of sleep, our journey stopping and starting, I was completely disorientated. I no longer knew where Andeera was. When I came round I found myself inside a women's prison, alone in the confines of a narrow cell.

A night didn't pass without them taking me for questioning. I lost count of my interrogators. In total, I was there for twenty-seven days, nine of which I spent in solitary confinement. Once I was allowed to mix with the other inmates I got to know many of them, and began to feel less anxious. The most memorable was 'the pleasure broker' as she liked to be known. She was thrilled when I told her I was from Yemen, because it gave her a chance to use the Arabic she'd learned through her work. She told me that she used to arrange temporary weddings, according to the terms of Shia doctrine, with 'a little independent judgement,' as she put it.

'I got so knowledgeable about sharia that I'd reached the level where I could make my own judgements,' she added, laughing. The Iranian authorities hadn't taken too kindly to this and accused her of sponsoring adultery.

There were other women there who I'll never forget: Jehad, a drug addict; Catherine, an American Israeli journalist; Shireen, who the authorities accused of provocation against the Islamic regime of Iran. She had removed her headscarf during an opposition demonstration and made a statement to a British newspaper professing her love for a young man from Iran's Jewish community. She admitted that, for her part, she would have no objection to marrying him.

Shireen told me: 'My problem isn't with the Iranian authorities, the worst they can do is kill us – and as you can see we're like the living dead anyway. My problem is with the young Jew who, unlike me, didn't dare admit that he wanted to marry me.' Then she added: 'He couldn't – couldn't even openly say he wanted to. At the beginning he wrote me a letter, telling me how much he loved me. Then he begged me to give it back, afraid someone else would read it, all the time saying he still loved me. But after a while he stopped telling me he loved me. It was like he was scared even of the walls, as though the walls had ears. He started looking at me in a certain way to tell me he loved me. But at the same time his eyes kept glancing at others – people crossing the street or sitting behind windows, or on the roofs of the cafes – scared that someone was watching us, or that someone might see us together.'

Every time I met her, Shireen retold her story, as though she wanted me to commit it to memory. She seemed certain I would leave the prison, taking her story with me. She was more confident of my release than of her own: 'Despite all the obstacles and the secrecy, I believed his love was real, and I felt the same. If I get out of this prison alive, the first thing I'll do is visit his grave. He committed suicide when he heard I'd been arrested. Perhaps he was afraid they'd come for him, afraid I'd give his name away and they'd arrest him too. Even though, truth be told, he'd been under arrest his whole short life; fear had kept him imprisoned all along. He could never be free of it, even in death. He never gave a reason for his suicide, so he never escaped.'

On the first night, my interrogators' questions focussed on why I had visited Afghanistan. They wanted the names of everyone I knew.

I soon got used to the interrogations, and learnt how to organise my thoughts so I could answer most of the questions – the same questions were posed in many different ways – without giving anything away. It seemed my interrogators were absolutely convinced I was one of Osama Bin Laden's wives. Time and time again I denied any connection to Bin Laden, but they were unshakeable in their conviction. Finally, a man arrived who said the Iranian authorities had agreed to release me and he'd been sent by the Yemeni embassy to repatriate me to Sana'a.

I'll stop here for a moment. I'd like to just listen to the song.

> His message was a path to the light
> His horses rode forth in the cause of right.

In the small bag Abu Abdullah had left in my care, I found exactly $34,620. Abu Abdullah had paid a year's rent up front on our house, so the money was plenty for me to live on for the next five years, maybe more. But I wanted to live with my family – with my mother, my father and my sister.

It had been over a year since I'd last heard from Abu Abdullah when my brother 'Abd al-Raqeeb returned from Chechnya. He brought with him a new wife, Valentina.

The home that 'Abd al-Raqeeb returned to was not the one he'd left. Everything had changed. Now it was not only a lonely place, but the very embodiment of loneliness.

One morning, around six months before his return, Mother had left the house to visit her brother's sick wife. Father left soon after her, but Lula said she wouldn't be going into work that day – she was going to see a girlfriend and would be back soon. I was left alone in the house. I'd refused to go with Mother as I still didn't really feel like talking to anyone. About an hour and a half later, Lula came home. I opened the door and she asked me to go and sit in Father's room. 'I've got a guest with me – I'll sit with her in our room,' she said, gesturing that I should go ahead of her.

From time to time, I could hear Lula's laughter coming from the next room, but her guest didn't make a sound.

I must have been dozing for a good while, when a knock on the door woke me. I got up to answer it. It was Father, home from work earlier than usual. He lay down on his bed, complaining of a sharp pain in his side. I knew this meant his kidney pains were back. He couldn't have an operation on them because of his weak heart.

'Lula's back home early, then?' he said when he heard her laughter.

'She's got a friend with her, someone from work I think.'

He twisted in discomfort, clutching his side. 'Take me to the bathroom. Ahh . . .' I placed his right arm over my shoulder and slid my left arm around his back to pull him up. I took his weight as he walked. As we made our way down the hallway he suddenly stopped in front of the door to our room, and said, 'I heard a man's voice.'

I hadn't heard anything, so I said, 'What man? There's no one there. It's just Lula and her friend.' But he straightened up, brushed aside my hands and banged on the door with surprising strength. The locked door, unaccustomed to such attack, flew open.

A terrible sight greeted him. My father stared in complete shock. For my part, I couldn't believe what I was seeing either. Had I known, I would never have answered the door to my father without warning Lula first. True, I never would have gone along with it if she'd told me who her guest really was, but she should have told me in any case. I'd just assumed her guest was a girl from work.

The sight of two naked bodies, in his home, in a state of intimate embrace, was too much for my father. Until he actually saw Lula's face he couldn't believe one of the bodies was his daughter's. Lula, paralysed by shame, was unable to hide her nakedness.

He taught us how to gain glory
So that we took command of the land by force.

The young man, taking advantage of my father's state of shock, bunched his clothes around his waist and fled from the room. I was astonished to see a woman's abaya tucked under his arm. I recalled seeing the form of a woman in a black abaya standing beside Lula when I opened the door and realised that the young man must have entered the house in disguise.

Father looked utterly broken. He just stood there, incapable of punishing Lula, incapable of speaking. He got his voice back after I gave him a glass of water. 'How could something like this happen in my own home? The home that I've worked all my life to strengthen with religious values and morals? How could my daughter, who I trusted, do such a thing? And you! You who have studied religion, and travelled to the ends of the earth to make jihad in the cause of God, you're OK with this?'

'No, Daddy, I'm not OK with this! I swear to you, in the name of God, the Almighty, I didn't know. She told me she had a friend with her and I saw a figure in an abaya, so I left them to come in by themselves. I didn't know it was a man under the abaya. On your life, Daddy! You mean everything to us!'

'To top it off, she brings him in wearing a woman's abaya! Something tells me this isn't the first time she's done this. You're swearing on my life, on your love for me, but what's life, what's love? I never thought, never once imagined, that my dignity would come to mean so little that it could be thrown away like this.'

Lula had put her clothes back on. She approached Father, who was lying on the living room floor, and attempted to console him: 'Daddy, you could never have expected it. You've known life's hardships, but you've never known how to overcome them.' As she came closer to him and he heard her words his anger flared up again. 'You've got the nerve to say that, even now? What hardships? What solutions? You — you whore! My daughter, a whore? This can't be happening.'

'I've never done anything that hasn't been for the sake of the family.'

'What? What are you saying?' Father was gasping now, struggling to speak. Lula went on: 'That's the truth, Daddy. Don't you be angry with me! Why now? Why is it OK for you to judge me now? Why didn't you judge and call me a whore when I was whoring myself to make money? You turned a blind eye because I was spending it on you. But now there's no more money, you've finally chosen to open your eyes.'

When I motioned for her to shut up, she got even more furious. 'Get lost, dimwit! You haven't got a clue what you're talking about!' she snapped.

I shot my hand out to cover her mouth. Father wasn't saying anything, just groaning in pain. Try as I might, I couldn't silence her, so I screamed at her 'Shut up! What's wrong with you? Have you lost it completely?!' Then Lula shoved my hand away – the sight of my father writhing in agony had finally hit home. 'I love you, Daddy. I didn't mean to hurt you. But what was I supposed to do? I wanted to do this one final thing. For me. But you had to come home early.'

Father was silent; he'd even stopped groaning. Was he in so much pain that he couldn't speak, or was he just ignoring her? It was Lula who realised, after she'd frantically checked his vital signs, that the reason he hadn't heard her was because he was dead.

Demands are not met by wishing
The world can only be won through struggle.

'Abd al-Raqeeb asked how Father had died. 'It was God's will,' Mother told him.

Lula and I hadn't told Mother the details of what had

happened, as we were scared she'd react in the same way as Father had.

Lula stopped going to work, and she no longer even left the house at all. She'd never been in such a bad way before, and only I knew the reason – although at first I wasn't completely sure. I kept asking myself if Lula was suffering guilt over Father's death? Or was it resentment? Resentment that all she'd done for us – or, as she put it, all 'the sweat of her pussy' she'd poured into making sure we never went hungry or lacked anything – had gone unappreciated?

After a week of Lula's ramblings, I realised her suffering actually had nothing to do with regret or guilt. It was as if her image of Father hadn't really changed at all, like nothing had even happened to him, or that what had happened had no significance. In a tone that was neither sorrowful nor bitter, and without a trace of irony, she would say that Father had known life's hardships, but he'd never known how to overcome them.

'True, he never just gave up, but then, neither did he do anything about his problems. What did him in was waiting for others to step up and solve them all for him. He was complacent, he never put himself out, never even thought how he might make things better. It made him passive. He did nothing, and he was nothing.'

Abu al-Zahra, I've overstepped my rank
In praising you, yet I seek the honour

Valentina seemed older than 'Abd al-Raqeeb. She was more feminine than his ex-wife Nura, and everything about her was glamorous. With Valentina, 'Abd al-Raqeeb was reborn a third time. As a young bachelor he'd been zealous to the point of extremism about his Marxist ideals and atheist opinions. Then after marrying Nura his jealously sent him to the other extreme, joining a jihadi group in a religious fervour and plotting to kill anyone he considered an infidel.

On the odd rare occasion 'Abd al-Raqeeb used to say to me – and to me alone – 'I have an important meeting with the group today.' But his group was no longer what it had been. With Valentina's arrival my brother burnt everything connected to the group: all of the books, pamphlets and cassettes that had filled his room. It was exactly like that other time when he was newly married and he burnt his Marxist books and his cassettes of socialist revolutionary songs.

'Abd al-Raqeeb resurrected his old motto, 'Playing in stoppage time is like playing outside the main game of life.' So, as he said, there was now nothing to tie him to the jihadi group. 'Perhaps it's like Bin Laden and his associates assumed their roles when it was time for them to play the game. And even if they did lose in the end, what matters is that they played. But those who came later, it looks like they chose to play in stoppage time. It just wasn't their time.'

The first time I heard him ask 'Where's the group?' I was puzzled, but I soon realised that he'd started referring to Valentina as 'The Group.' She had became his group, his creed. He still claimed to follow Imam Abu Hanifa's school of Islamic law, which his new wife also belonged to. But it would have been more honest if he'd told us he'd become a follower of Valentina.

'My Communist parents named me after Valentina, a Russian space pioneer of the Soviet era,' she explained to

us the day she arrived at our home. Lula looked at her
with envy in her eyes. 'Valentina the Russian was free to
go all the way up into space,' she observed, 'but you, you
can't even go up to the roof of the house – if you tried,
just once, like Nura did, you'd be hit by the busybodies'
missiles and burnt by the flames of gossip. You'd be taken
out by a hidden camera.'

Valentina described herself as a nationalist mujahid,
rather than a religious mujahid, but maintained she wasn't
a Communist like her family all were. Despite this, 'Abd
al-Raqeeb continued to insist that she followed the school
of Abu Hanifa.

Valentina filled 'Abd al-Raqeeb's life with affection. So
much so that he overflowed with it. Lula thought she was
a fake, and never really got on with her. Valentina clearly
took an interest in her appearance, but above all she was
concerned with 'Abd al-Raqeeb's meals, clothes, comfort,
and peace of mind. She even made sure he smelled nice
(how could it be that he had started using scent, when he'd
been such a stranger to it before?). Despite the obvious
power of her beauty, Valentina never faltered in her boundless obedience to our brother. Perhaps it was this behavior
that made 'Abd al-Raqeeb so defenceless before her, telling
her 'Don't ask, Valentina, command me. You're going to
have everything you want.' But, as Lula saw it, her behaviour had just one motivation, a motivation that she alone
had observed. In a whisper she told me that Valentina had
discovered the secret of our brother's strength, which Nura
had failed to recognise.

'Your brother didn't go to fight against the Russians
alongside the Chechen mujahideen, he went to raid
Chechnya itself. He drew his sword and conquered one of

Chechnya's women – an impressive conquest – and then returned home victorious.'

No man can claim eloquence
Unless he finds its source in you.

I have praised kings and risen high in their esteem
But when I praise you I rise above the clouds.

I followed the news closely, listening for updates on the mujahideen in Afghanistan and Guantanamo Bay, hoping to find out if Abu Abdullah was still alive. But after more than a year and a half of waiting I still hadn't heard anything, so I decided to return to university.

At some point after Father's death we'd acquired a television and video player. We also now used our mobile phones openly. Yet, in spite of this, I felt that my life was stuck between the four walls, even when I was walking down the street or at the market. University also began to seem oppressive. But its walls were thick, walls that embodied everything walls represent. Something about this drew me to them. I tried to reclaim them, as though I were trying to reclaim myself, or draw closer to myself. But I was no longer the person I used to be, even if I hadn't become a different person.

I have praised kings and risen high in their esteem
But when I praise you I rise above the clouds.

Lula's depression was deepening, and despite our best efforts, it seemed we could do nothing to help her. 'Abd al-Raqeeb's trading business was making a good profit and he and

Valentina bought a house, where they were spared the melancholic atmosphere of our home. As is the custom, when Mother died they moved back and spent forty days with us. They were clearly relieved when the time was up and they were able to return to their own home.

It was just Lula and I in the house now. I was in my third year of university. She kept saying she had no regrets, that she couldn't have done things any other way. Still, she often spoke about Mother and Father's marriage, her voice heavy with nostalgia.

'They continued to live together after they got old. They reminisced about their youth and their past. But me, I have nothing worth remembering. Faces, the things I've done and said, pass through my memory like fragments of a dream or some terrifying nightmare. They float like bubbles and, try as I might, I just can't catch them.' Then she'd fall silent for a while and simply look at me.

'Do you think I made a mistake by bringing that young man home? I'm getting old and I'm not as desirable as I used to be. Can you believe that I sewed up my pussy twice? The last time I did it so I'd look like a virgin for someone who only wanted to sleep with virgins. But even then, no one wanted me. Then I was afraid that on the Day of Judgement I'd meet my Lord as a virgin and he'd put me with the virtuous virgins. I was worried, I didn't want to cheat God. So as soon as that young man looked at me in the street, I acknowledged him. He was obedient, willing, like it was his first time. I arranged to meet him later. He came to me wearing the abaya, just as I'd asked him. This was my plan to get what I wanted, needed . . . for the last time.'

I didn't want to risk her getting too worked-up, so I'd just listen without commenting. She was no longer fully aware of her behaviour. She'd spend her time watching porn – or cultural films as she still called them – and listening to religious cassettes. Sometimes, she'd remember to pray, even without making her ablutions first, or while she had her period.

As she became more and more disturbed she stopped eating and would refuse all my attempts to feed her. One night, seeing how frail she was made me so anxious that I couldn't sleep. I called 'Abd al-Raqeeb and asked him to come over; but he and Valentina were too late. By the time they arrived, Lula's stubbornness had won out – she'd killed herself with hunger and exhaustion.

I pray to God for the children of my religion
May He hear and grant my prayers

'Abd al-Raqeeb decided to sell me the share of our house he'd inherited. It was a nominal sale and no money was ever actually exchanged. He saw it as his gift to me. He and Valentina tried to persuade me to move in with them, but I insisted on staying put, alone with my memories.

By the time I'd reached my final year of university I'd become fixated on what might have happened to Abu Abdullah, and I couldn't concentrate on my studies. I needed answers so that I could find some peace of mind. One day, I was reading the student newspaper when I noticed the name of the Islamic education professor who'd lectured us in my first year, before I dropped out. He had a column where he answered readers' questions on various points of sharia. Next to his name was his email address.

I'd heard and read about the internet, but I'd never used it. Hefsa, who I knew from class, was happy to teach me how. We found an internet café and I sat beside her in front of one of the computers. 'It's simple . . .' she began.

The very next day I had an internet connection installed and bought an 'Islamic' computer, as it was described on the box. When you switched it on you weren't greeted with the usual start-up tone, instead you were treated to the bismillah, the standard Muslim invocation – 'In the name of God, the Most Gracious, the Most Merciful . . .' – and a verse from the Quran: 'Glory to Him Who has subjected this to our use . . .' In fact, all the audio notifications took the form of a Quranic verse.

'Dear Sheikh Abu Surur,
Peace be upon you and God's mercy and blessings, and may He reward you for the fatwas you have issued, illuminating for us the path of Islam.
    Five years ago I had the honour of being one of your students. I was at that time in the first year of my studies, before I interrupted them. I am writing to ask you to answer my query and direct me to a solution that will please God, may He be glorified and exalted. Since my query is of a personal nature I would ask you to send me your telephone number so that I can contact you and explain. Peace be upon you and God's mercy and blessings.'

This was the first email I'd ever sent.

He got back to me, and I called him.

'What is the opinion of the merciful law, dear Sheikh, if a man disappears during war and his wife doesn't hear from him for more than four years? Does she remain under his custody as his wife, even though she doesn't know whether he's dead or alive?'

'No, no, no.' I didn't know what he meant.

'What do you mean, our Sheikh?'

'Listen, it depends on the circumstances. Come to the Islamic Guidance Centre tomorrow, after the afternoon prayer, and explain the problem to me in more detail. I'll tell my secretary to make sure I see you first.'

I went to the centre. It must have been his own private centre since I was alone in front of him, trying to avoid his scrutinising gaze.

'No, no. It is not permitted that you remain in his custody. Islam is ease, not hardship,' he said.

He issued his fatwa before I'd even finished explaining the problem. Had his eyes uncovered the details of the problem as they stared at my body, wrapped in the abaya and veil? 'Jihad is a duty, but . . .' He was silent for a moment before continuing, as though he'd wanted to give a smile as a preface to what he was about to say, 'How can they go off to jihad, when there are things right here that need jihad? Didn't the poet say:

"They say, go out in jihad, Jameel, do battle

But what jihad could I want beside women?"'

I remembered what Lula had once said about jihad, something which had sounded like a line of poetry. I also remembered the same professor's lecture. In the first year his words had come as a surprise to us, but what he said now somehow seemed less surprising.

Not only did he help me by issuing a fatwa, but he also promised to accompany me to see a lawyer. He even insisted that he would be by my side when, four months after first seeing the lawyer, my case was heard at the

Personal Status Court. After some questioning and investigation, the judge ruled that I was officially divorced from
my husband, whose fate remained unknown.

That day I went home feeling as though a great weight
had been lifted from my shoulders, a dead weight, or a
living weight – no one knew. It was the worst burden I'd
ever carried, for there had been no possibility of relief.

After this the sheikh took the initiative and called to ask
me to meet him at the centre the following morning. I
didn't think to question the motive behind his invitation,
instead my thoughts were full of the poetry he'd recited
during our first meeting.

During my early years at school I was in love with
poetry. I memorised many poems, the ones we studied at
school and the collections 'Abd al-Raqeeb used to give me.
If I've used any poetic words or turns of phrase in this
confession of mine, it's as a result of my early passion for
reading. I used to pen my poetic musings in literature class,
but the teacher kept telling me off for being overly fanciful,
for having too much imagination. She censored the first
story I wrote without even telling me why.

I didn't sleep well after he called me that evening. All
my senses burned with the thought of jihad – not the jihad
I'd known and lived, but the kind of jihad I'd known only
in films and the Prophet's sayings. I remembered what Lula
had said about 'Abd al-Raqeeb's jihad and his conquest of
Valentina.

'Who will make jihad for my cause and conquer me,
and when?' I asked Lula, crying as I remembered her.

When I got to the centre the secretary wasn't at his

desk so I went straight to the sheikh's office and knocked on the door. He invited me in.

'We usually open in the evenings but I wanted us to meet in a more relaxed, less formal atmosphere,' he explained as he fished out a carton of mango juice from a draw inside his desk and offered it to me. 'Drink in good health. There's nothing else in the office. Please take it.'

I was confused. How could I drink in front of him without taking my veil off? Wouldn't this go against sharia, at least according to what we'd learned at university, where he'd been one of our professors?

'Thank you, but I don't want to drink mango just now.' I'd wanted to tell him indirectly that I could drink mango juice, but there was a legal prohibitive that meant I couldn't drink it under these particular circumstances.

'Only an ingrate refuses an invitation to drink,' he said, waiting for me to comply. So I moved the mango carton up behind my veil towards my mouth, assuming this is how he expected me to drink it. But before I could take a sip he said, 'Remove your veil. Don't be scared. I am your teacher and sheikh, after all, and are you not a divorcee now? Perhaps . . . Perhaps . . .' He coughed out a laugh, and continued, 'I might find you pleasing, and then perhaps marry you in accordance with God's law and the example of His Prophet.'

I felt as though time, all time – everything I'd lived through and all that lay ahead of me – was spinning through my head and all around it, like a sudden storm. I could never have anticipated this; I, who'd married Abu Abdullah before he'd even opened his eyes to see my face. Confused and embarrassed, I felt myself responding to his request. But there was something else, something I felt deep within me. It pushed me past my embarrassment, to reveal more than he'd asked for: I removed both my headscarf and my veil, and I shook my hair loose.

'God bless! God bless!' he exclaimed in astonishment as he rose from his desk. He came over and sat in front of me, leaning into my face, which seemed to have excited him: 'Listen, I'll give you whatever dowry you want. You're divorced, a free woman. We just have to agree to get married, you don't need permission from your legal male guardian.'

'So fast! Please be a little patient. I need to think it over first,' I said, finding it all too much too soon.

Back home, I thought it over and over but couldn't reach a decision, so I prayed the decision-making prayer, and found myself agreeing.

'There's no time. Just say yes. One word from you and you'll become my wife in the eyes of sharia,' he said when I went to see him the next day.

I gave him what he wanted and from that moment on I became obedient to him, as a hurma, naturally.

We went to complete the formalities with a religious judge the sheikh knew, in the presence of witnesses he'd called up who met us there. Afterwards he took me to an apartment building which he said he owned. It had six floors. At the door to one of the flats he pulled out a key and gave it to me: 'Go on, open it. It's yours.' Everything looked as though it had been carefully prepared, not least the bedroom. The bed itself was alluring, seeming to promise a night of unbridled frolics.

He took a carton from a little fridge in the corner beside the bed. By the time I'd finished in the bathroom he was licking the last of the carton's contents from a spoon.

I was pretty sure it was a mixture of honey and strengthening herbs like Abu Abdullah used to take.

Contrary to my expectations, my new husband jumped
on top of me. He pulled off his clothes and helped me out
of what little I was still wearing. Wasting no time, he began
to kiss me on the lips and suck my tongue.

He aroused me like I'd never been aroused before. He
drove me wild with his kisses on my neck, breasts and
between my thighs. I writhed against his mouth, gasping
in pleasure. I was elated. What I was experiencing was
something I'd never known or even come close to before.
I said to myself, 'God is compensating me.'

As my excitement became almost unbearable, I found
myself trying to guide him in, opening myself up for him
to enter me.

He responded by pressing his thing into me. He continued
to aim his blows at the door, but they were more like slaps
of flaccid meat, like the offal you can buy from the butchers,
all slack intestines that had never known an erection.

I felt such intense frustration it was more like anger
and disgust. I noticed the white of his thick beard showing
despite the patches of henna he'd tried to cover it up with.
I hadn't noticed the white before or any of the other signs
of ageing he had concealed with his fake smile, like more
henna. I wanted to smash his head with something hard
and solid, but I could only find the carton he had tried to
treat his impotency with. Before I could do anything, he
noticed my anger and tried to placate me, saying:

'I thought I'd overcome the weakness. I wanted to get
married, to try again. But now it's your right to ask for a
divorce. You are free. You are free. You are free. I'll do
anything you ask, my daughter.'

What could I have possibly wanted from him other than what I'd thought was finally within my grasp? It looked like he was trying to force a smile to accompany the words that were coming out of his mouth, but his impotency now exposed, this was no longer possible. He could only twist his mouth into a frown.

By saying 'you are free' three times he had effectively divorced me. And by calling me his 'daughter' this meant I was now like a daughter to him. Mother used to say a woman's freedom was subject to her male guardian – father, brother or husband. If a man tells his wife she is free three times then according to tradition this means she's divorced and no longer his wife.

I'd wanted to say these words to him, to divorce him myself, but he had pre-empted me.

In times of trouble and adversity
You are the Muslims' sole refuge.

What happened between the sheikh and I was no different to how a piece of chewing gum is treated. In one hour, or less than that, I'd become a stick of chewing gum. He'd squashed me between his teeth, chewed me for a few minutes to taste my sweetness on his tongue, and then spat me out.

But those few minutes had been enough to reignite desires I'd thought long buried.

I tried to pray to God as often as I could. I prayed the 'prayer of need,' despite what I'd heard about it being an innovation. I needed a man. I needed to live, to taste life . . . Just to taste it.

I prayed to God, but He didn't answer. I became more

and more frustrated as the days went by – in fact with every hour and every second.

I tried to get my life in order. I asked myself: What do I want, and how am I going to get it?

But my inner turmoil made it impossible to get anything in order, never mind working out what I actually wanted. The way I saw it, there was just one thing I needed, one thing I really desired. This desire needed an outlet, more so than my need for order. I remembered Andeera and what she'd said about transcending emotions and desire, and how, without them, we can live in inner peace. But how could there be inner peace with the unquenchable flames of desire? Weren't Andeera's words just a tranquilliser or a temporary fix? All I could feel inside me were the fires of war that defeated any peace and consumed everything with their flames. A fire that, once lit, could not be extinguished.

Demands are not met

I graduated from university and started teaching Islamic education at a private school.

Most of my female colleagues were spinsters. There were no male teachers, no one I could have pursued or fulfilled my desires with.

Had I changed?

Yes, I'd changed. To be honest, I'd grown tired of dreaming about finding a man. I spent most of my time – days and nights, asleep and awake – dreaming of a man, a man to hold me tight, to make love to me until I cried out in pleasure. I began to tell myself that God is forgiving, and merciful, and that he will forgive me the one sin I was going to commit in my whole life. If I couldn't be married according to God's law and the example of His Prophet, then I had no choice but to commit a sin. Just once. Just this once.

The nearest man to our house was Suhail. I felt he was the only suitable man out of our neighbours who was likely to respond to my advances. After all, hadn't he given me the Om Kalthoum song?

His house was just six metres from ours. He and his wife had lived alone there since his parents had gone back to live in their village and his only sister had got married.

He was a member of the National Orchestra and must have been in his forties. He had married twice. Then he had divorced his first wife after they'd had four children together. He visited their mother every month, and contributed as much as he could afford towards their school fees. The second had left their only child with her mother and travelled to Morocco where she was writing her PhD on the modern Yemeni novel.

I searched and found the number for his landline written on the kitchen wall. I couldn't believe my luck when I also found his mobile phone number.

Mother used to call his wife whenever she needed something. She'd written down Suhail's mobile number so she could contact her through him, before they'd had a landline installed.

I began to bombard him with messages from my mobile, the same one I'd had for over five years. I'd begin by showering him with praise, describing him as a great musician who should be recognised for his talents, and always adding, 'This is not just empty praise.'

I didn't tell him my name, and he never seemed interested in finding out, or even in taking any initiative to bring us together, like asking me to meet him or calling me to hear my voice – to make sure I was a female, a real woman, and not just an illusion. His replies were curt, usually just a single word, such as 'Hello!' or 'Thanks,' unless I asked him something that required a more substantial response.

Apart from his daily habit of chewing khat, and the boisterous late nights he spent in the company of his musician friends from time to time, everything about him suggested he was a perfectly respectable member of society. Even so, both Father and 'Abd al-Raqeeb had decided he was a libertine.

Once I messaged him: 'Don't you long, you wonderful artist, for a woman to sit by your side. Don't you desire a female? How have you been able to live without a woman since your wife left?'

He answered 'I have a woman from another world, an invisible woman who visits me whenever I need her.'

I decided to go to him, to become a fantasy woman, or at least try to appear as one. I put on my make-up and sprayed myself with perfume. I did everything I could to charm the eye and beguile the nose. I thought of all the things that might arouse a man, and I went to him. When he opened the door I pulled the veil from my face and opened the curtain that hid my fancy clothes. 'I am Laylat al-Qadr, the Night of Destiny,' I said to him.

'Welcome, Laylat al-Qadr, better than a thousand months. Better than a thousand women.'

I thought he meant to invite me in. Perhaps I believed I really was Laylat al-Qadr who we learned was better than a thousand months. Every year, she came down from the heavens on this night, on the twenty-seventh of Ramadan, and granted the wishes of whoever set eyes on her.

'Can't I come in?' I said to him, still standing at the door.

'You can't. I'm by myself, there aren't any women at home.'

'You'll regret it,' I said to him as though I really were Laylat al-Qadr.

I returned wretched and alone to the house, the streets and markets bustling on a Ramadan night like no other.

Nothing is beyond the reach of a people

He hadn't realised I was his neighbour, so then why hadn't he welcomed me in as a fantasy woman, like the one who comes to him from another world, as he'd put it? Didn't I tell him I was Laylat al-Qadr? I could no longer suppress or hide my desire. It intruded upon my every thought, my every word. I became painfully aware of this when I asked the bus driver to stop so I could get off. Instead of saying the usual, 'Please, stop here', I said 'Please, fuck me,' to the astonishment of the other passengers and the embarrassment of the driver who seemed to have understood what I'd wanted to say and stopped the bus for me to get off.

The B-side . . . The A-side

Ask my heart when it comes to its senses
Perhaps it will hold beauty to blame.

Ask a sensible man for sensible answers
But who could keep his wits in the face of such beauty?

If I were to ask my heart
Tears would answer in its place.

In my chest there is only flesh and blood
Feeble now that youth has gone.

My heart weeps and I say: It's over
In my chest it trembles and I say: Come to!

I thought I knew this part of the song well, so it was only
when I read the words of the original poem the song is
based on, in a book, that I realised my mistake. I became
obsessed with the poem. At first I looked for it in the
collected works of the poet Ahmed Shawqi, but it wasn't
there. Finally, I managed to find it in some books on Om

Kalthoum, and in a couple of old volumes that included excerpts of Shawqi's poetry. It turned out I'd been mishearing one of the words, and there were two different versions. When I compared the published version of the poem with what I heard Om Kalthoum singing over Riyad al-Sunbati's music I realised the word at the end of the first and tenth lines wasn't what I'd thought it was. Up until then I'd heard the very familiar word *taaba*, meaning 'repent' but it was actually a classical Arabic word I didn't know, *thaaba*, that I found out from the the dictionary means something like 'come to' or 'recover one's senses.'

But was Om Kalthoum really singing *thaaba*? Didn't the lyrics reproduced in the Om Kalthoum biography I'd found have it as *taaba*, just as I'd heard it all along? Maybe now I'd read Shawqi's original words I was just hearing it differently? Ah, when she sings these lines they get me every time:

My heart weeps and I say: It's over
In my chest it trembles and I say: Come to!

When Om Kalthoum sings *duloo* – 'chest' – her voice trembles like it's overflowing with *everything* – every imaginable and unimaginable thing. That word . . . I'm spellbound by it, it blows me away . . . It makes me feel like I'm losing my mind.

In my chest it trembles and I say: Come to!

I checked and *duloo* wasn't one of the ninety-nine beautiful names of God. But when Om Kalthoum sang it, it sounded as though it should be.

For me, *duloo* became every name, even my own, which I could no longer recall after I'd been abbreviated by my designation as a 'hurma.' Hurma – the word that replaced me. But wasn't I a hurma before I became a hurma? How could this word replace me then, when I was a hurma from the very beginning?

When their feet are firmly in the stirrups

Perhaps I could have pursued another man, but even the thought of getting close to anyone – any man who wasn't Suhail – made me feel that I'd become some sort of deviant, a whore who didn't care who she had sex with. I was afraid of scandal. I was afraid people would label me as a whore. I considered adopting another name, of going with the first man who flirted with me in the street, but I remembered what I'd heard about the police raiding some homes on the pretext that they were 'dens of iniquity.' Sometimes they simply arrested any couple they found together, be it in a car, restaurant or garden. Even if it turned out they were actually married, they'd only release them after a thorough investigation.

I even visited the neighbourhood's famous matchmaker who had found husbands for countless young girls. It was obvious her words were meant for me when she said: 'Men, whether they're young or old, it doesn't matter – they all want you to find them young bribes, usually between fourteen and seventeen years old.'

My best bet was to get closer to Suhail. But this looked like it was going to be difficult, if not impossible. I said to myself that it would be easier for me to become a whore and expose myself to the world. But this was just me looking for excuses not to go through with my plan.

I would dig a tunnel from our house to his. I would take a pick and shovel and start digging. The tunnel wouldn't need to be longer than, say, ten metres to get me into Suhail's house, or to be more precise, his kitchen, which he hadn't used since his wife left for Morocco. I'd keep the dirt in sacks and dig the tunnel three metres deep. Obviously, I'd need to make the tunnel wide enough for me to fit through it.

I came down with a nasty cough and couldn't dig for a few days. But I soon got back to work.

I reckoned it would take four months to dig the tunnel, more or less. Towards the end, I'd tunnel upwards and pop up in the musician's kitchen. When I got nearer to Suhail's house I would only dig in the mornings, when he was at work, so that he wouldn't hear the sound of the pick and shovel.

I'd have to wear something over my clothes to keep them clean and pretty for when I revealed myself to him.

And then what?

Would he be scared this time? Would there be a look of terror on his face when he saw me?

Would he scream 'Who are you?'

I'll say, 'I am a jinn. I have come to lay with you this night.'

'Who are you? Tell me the truth. I don't believe in jinns.'

'Whether or not you believe it, I am a jinn!'

At first he'll laugh, but then he'll quickly frown again and he'll growl, 'Get back to where you came from. No more of your nonsense. Go on!'

There'll be nothing I can do in the face of his pig-headedness, except of course to go back through the tunnel.

His indifference when I emerged from my tunnel would

be even more bizarre than my plan. But surely there had to be a reason for such indifference? Obviously, his love for his wife or his religious values just wouldn't allow it. But probably, the truth was that neither love nor religion mattered all that much to him.

He taught us how to gain glory
So that we took command of the land by force.

Were love and religion really not important to him?

If not, then why had he sent me the Om Kalthoum song that brought us together?

As the days passed I became more and more convinced Suhail was my destiny. I could no longer think of any other man, since this would be an adventure with consequences I couldn't even begin to imagine. I'm not Lula, who took her story to the grave.

I thought and thought about it until I decided to go to him again, to meet him face to face. I wore more make-up and perfume this time.

As soon as he opened the door I dived forward to embrace him.

He jumped back and stared at me. This time he recognised me.

'You're married.'

'I'm not married anymore. I'm divorced.'

'This isn't right.'

'It is right.'

I begged him, getting down on my knees and hugging his legs. I wanted to kiss his feet but he wouldn't give in, even though his thing was clearly erect, pushing up against the fabric of his *thobe*.

Crying, I pleaded with him: 'Just let me touch it. Pleeeeease . . . Let me just touch it. Don't deprive me of that. I'm begging you.'

He gave in to my hands as I pulled off his *thobe* and baggy cotton trousers. But when I tried to move closer to him he stepped back, putting his right hand to his left cheek – swollen with the ball of khat he had in his mouth – as though he were thinking. I howled and writhed. I sobbed and then I put it between my fingers again. I wanted to pull him deep inside me; but he began to ejaculate as soon as his thing even touched my clitoris, and it was over before it even began. It was as though Suhail had managed to keep his outrage in check until his imploring thing got what it wanted, but then he had to ask it to leave immediately.

Even if hearts were made of iron
Still none could bear what mine has suffered.

No one can tell you about life's hardships
Like someone who has lost their loved ones.

Before what happened happened, I found out I was pregnant. That's what the doctor told me.

Suhail's thing hadn't got any further than my clitoris, and he had ejaculated right there. So where had the baby come from?

Had the dregs of the sheikh's drips been all it took? But that was a good while ago. Was I doomed to have a baby from the limp cum of the sheikh or the musician? The doctor confirmed I was still a virgin. She laughed out loud when I told her I'd never slept with a man and that she was free to examine me.

I didn't know what to do. I was completely bewildered despite the momentary joy I'd feel whenever I imagined that a solid body would finally emerge from between my legs. It would push with palpable force from inside me, after I'd waited long years to feel such a force penetrate me from the outside.

Demands are not be won through struggle.
The world can only be won through struggle.

I made up my mind to leave with my baby, and get far away from the house and the lingering smells of its memories, which no longer meant anything to me. But as soon as I set foot outside, what happened happened. The thing I never thought would happen happened.

I saw him striding towards me, as though marching to a new battle.

The man I thought was dead had returned. Abu Abdullah had returned, and refused to recognise the divorce.

'Have you divorced me through an infidel court? This is not legitimate.'

In that moment, I wished I had a gun or a knife to put an end to him once and for all. I reminded him about Andeera, telling him, 'Send for Andeera, she's your wife.' He said that she was free now, since God had only used her to aid the mujahideen.

He tried to get 'Abd al-Raqeeb to convince me, but he was preoccupied with Valentina and business. This time around, he wasn't there to give his consent and impose on me the will of his old associate in jihad.

Nothing is beyond the reach of a people
When their feet are firmly in the stirrups.

I leave the house . . . I don't know where I'm going. I just want to get far away, away from myself, from where I was, from the memories, the familiar scents. I don't care where I go . . . I eat from rubbish and sleep in rubbish. I'm in a rubbish dump . . .A hurma in a rubbish dump . . .A rubbish dump in a hurma . . . I walk the streets . . . Walk and walk. People turn to stare. I'm free. I'm free. I'm a hurma. I'm a free hurma . . . I'm free and a hurma. I'm my own hurma . . .The hurma of my freedom . . . It's a hurma. It's a hurma and I'm someone else . . . I tear off my veil. I tear off my abaya and headscarf and walk on . . . I toss away the gold on my arms and neck . . . I undo the buttons of my blouse and shrug it off my shoulders. I pull my bra down to my belly. I chuck it to a cute dog to sniff. I can feel the wind on my breasts . . . I step out of my trousers. I walk. I keep walking. I walk without myself. I leave myself behind. I was a hurma and I became a hurma. I became a hurma without it meaning anything. A hurma without meaning. I was someone else and I became me. I was me and I became someone else. I was someone else and I became someone else.

Glossary

Ahmed Shawqi: Egyptian poet and dramatist, 1868-1932, known as the Prince of Poets, who introduced the genre of poetic epics to the Arabic literary tradition.

Ababil: birds, with the world's largest wings, said in the Quran to have come down from heaven to protect Mecca from the Habashi army by dropping red clay bricks on their elephants as they advanced on the city.

abaya: a voluminous black garment worn over other clothes by some Muslim women.

baltu: an ankle-length overcoat (from the French *paletot*).

duha, witr, and *tajahud* **prayers**: optional additional prayers made at specific times between the five obligatory daily prayers in Islam.

hadith: a saying of the Prophet Muhammad transmitted by established Islamic sources which, along with accounts of his daily practice (the Sunna), constitute the major source of guidance for Muslims apart from the Quran.

harem: historically a group of women all belonging to the same household and living segregated from the men.

Hurma: literally 'sanctity.' An entity to be protected from violation or dishonour, usually by a male guardian. The term implies ownership of the woman, and a lack of agency.

Jameela, Fatina, Ghaniya: three common women's names meaning Beautiful, Charming and Prosperous respectively.

jinn: a supernatural spirit appearing in pre-Islamic Arabian mythology as well as the Quran; of a lower rank than the angels, they are able to appear in human and animal forms and to possess humans.

khat: the leaves of the flowering shrub *Catha edulis*, native to the Arabian Peninsula and the Horn of Africa, the chewing of which is a long-established social custom in (mainly male) communities all around the Red Sea. It contains cathinone, an amphetamine-like stimulant, which is said to cause excitement, loss of appetite and euphoria.

Laylat al-Qadr: the night during the holy month of Ramadan when the first verses of the Quran were revealed to the Prophet Muhammad. As Layla, meaning night, is a common women's name, Hurma is imagining a seductive female personification of the holy event.

mujahid, mujahida, mujahideen: Islamic guerrilla fighter or Holy Warrior engaged in jihad (male, female and plural form of the noun).

Om Kalthoum: the most famous Arab singer of all time, known in Arabic as the Star of the East, loved for her long and intensely emotional live performances from the 1920s until her death in 1975.

Riyad al-Sunbati: Egyptian composer and lyricist, 1906-1981.

salam: literally 'peace,' used as a greeting or a farewell.

sheikh, sheikha: term of respect for an elder or a religious authority (male and female form of the noun).

thobe: a robe-like ankle-length man's cotton shirt worn by men across the Arabian Peninsula.